CALLED HOME

Also by Robert Irvine

Moroni Traveler mysteries

Gone to Glory
The Angels' Share
Baptism for the Dead

Other novels

Ratings Are Murder
Footsteps
The Devil's Breath
Horizontal Hold
The Face Out Front
Freeze Frame
Jump Cut

ROBERT IRVINE

ST. MARTIN'S PRESS

CALLED HOME

A THOMAS · DUNNE BOOK

NEW YORK

Design by Judith A. Stagnitto

Library of Congress Cataloging-in-Publication Data

Irvine, R. R. (Robert R.)
    Called home / Robert Irvine.
        p.   cm.
    "A Thomas Dunne book."
    ISBN 0-312-05829-2
    I. Title.
PS3559.R65C35   1991
813'.54—dc20   90-29267
                                                       CIP

10 9 8 7 6 5 4 3 2

To the memory of
David Charles Laertes Saltzman

"Always marry a girl from Sanpete,
because no matter how hard things get,
you'll know she has seen worse."

—*Early Mormon leader*

CALLED

HOME

O
N
E

His Honor, Magistrate Jim Doyle, was staring at Traveler
like a hanging judge fingering hemp.

Behind Traveler, his father coughed to show that he was
in his seat. Martin had been doing that all through the trial,
his way of letting Traveler know he wasn't alone.

The judge shifted his glare to Martin just as Mad Bill
added fuel to the fire with a cough fit for a TB sanitarium.
Without turning around, Traveler knew that Bill was seated
to one side of Martin, Charlie Redwine on the other. For
once, the pair of them, Salt Lake's Sandwich Prophet (so
called because of his sandwich board prophecies) and his
lone disciple, had traded their robes and Navajo charms for a
couple of Martin's suits.

Traveler was out of uniform, too, in an itchy blue wor-
sted dug from the back of his closet.

Don't scratch. Don't squirm. Think decorum at all times
while in court. Words of wisdom from Reed Critchlow, his

lawyer. Smile at the jury, but not too broadly. Look put upon, offended, but never concerned. Sit up straight. Keep good eye contact. Don't look evasive.

Traveler's Adam's apple bobbed against the knot in the first tie he'd worn in months. To the jury, he must look like some kind of salesman. Which was just what Critchlow wanted. Sell yourself. That's all I ask.

"Before we begin closing arguments," the judge said, "I'd like a conference please, gentlemen."

Critchlow and the prosecutor, a Mormon bishop named Oscar Young doing double duty as Assistant City Attorney, moved to the bench on the bailiff's side where they began a spirited three-way whisper.

Martin took the opportunity to murmur, "I took a case for you during recess, Moroni."

"You have a lot of faith," Traveler said over his shoulder, hoping the jury wouldn't feel slighted at being left out of the conversation. "I could be serving jail time by tonight."

"Stop trying to sound like a martyr," Martin said.

"Playing on our sympathy," Bill added.

"You heard what Critchlow said," Martin went on. "'There's no case against you. It's harassment, pure and simple.'"

"Countersue the bastards," Charlie said. "That's my advice."

Bill said, "You have enemies in the land of Zion. There's no other explanation for what's happening to you."

Traveler had heard it all before, words of comfort from father, friends, and attorney alike. But he was still sitting there in the defendant's chair.

"We've got bail money in case you need it," Bill whispered.

Traveler snorted. "You said there was nothing to worry about."

"You heard your lawyer," Martin said, trying to sound

brash. "There's absolutely no chance of conviction." But
Traveler knew his father too well to miss the concern in his
voice. A felony conviction meant loss of license, and an end
to their two-man private investigating firm.

.Yet the charge against him was exactly what Critchlow
had said, harassment instigated by his former lady friend,
Claire Bennion, and propagated by an overzealous policeman
who wanted to rid Brigham Young's promised land of yet another Gentile, the term applying to the likes of Traveler and
all non-Mormons.

No Gentiles in heaven, he'd been told since he was a boy.
No sinning heathens like yourself.

At the moment, his only earthly sin was defending himself against one of Claire's vendettas. If he hadn't fought
back, he'd have been the one in the hospital.

"This client I mentioned," Martin said. "His case is just
what you need to get your mind off that woman."

Traveler fought a losing battle to keep his eyes off her.
Claire was sitting less than ten feet away, directly behind the
prosecutor's desk. She'd been perched there since the trial
began. Smiling, gloating even. Thinner than ever, needing a
man to feed upon. But still attractive enough to turn the
heads of the jury every time she rearranged her extraordinary
legs.

Both lawyers took their places. The judge cleared his
throat. "Ladies and gentlemen of the jury, I apologize. We're
going to take another short recess. I find I have a previous
commitment concerning another case." He glanced at the
clock. "Please be back in your seats at half past the hour."

Traveler sighed as the jurors hurried out of court. If they
wanted to smoke, they'd have to go all the way outside in
this Mormon Country, where Joseph Smith's Word of
Wisdom declared tobacco one of the deadliest of sins.

He stole another glance at Claire. She hadn't budged.
And wouldn't unless he did. Then she'd follow him, to the

door of the men's room if that's where he headed. All the while smiling enigmatically.

Critchlow, one of Martin's cronies who was giving Traveler a break on legal fees, shuffled papers and spoke under his breath. "Smile at her, for Christ's sake."

Traveler wet his lips.

"If you can't smile, don't look at her."

Traveler shifted his gaze to one of the City and County Building's narrow Gothic windows. The building, which took up an entire block, had recently been refurbished to full Victorian splendor, its sandstone facade of gargoyles, priests, and politicians no longer falling on passersby below.

"I'm going for a pee," Critchlow said. "How about you?"

"I'm fine."

"I don't want you squirming during the summations."

"Trust me."

The lawyer shrugged and left the courtroom.

Traveler went back to staring out the window. A wind shift started ash raining from the sky, fallout from a forest fire burning along the Mormon Trail where it came down Emigration Canyon east of town. It had been burning for days, following the pioneer route and closing in on the suburbs, fed by the heat of an Indian summer.

"You're late," Martin said.

Traveler turned in time to see his friend and landlord, Barney Chester, slide onto the wooden bench next to Charlie. Chester had an unlit cigar clamped between his teeth. He took it out to say, "Hey, Mo, your client has arrived and is waiting in my office even as we speak."

"What client?"

Martin sighed dramatically. "I told you I'd accepted a case for you. Signed and sealed."

"I like to meet my clients." Traveler closed his eyes. When he opened them, Martin was doing his best to smile. But it was lip service only. The rest of his face looked as nervous as Traveler felt. Even so, there'd been no recriminations about Claire from his father. They'd both been suckered too many times for that, though in Traveler's case, his attitude toward her defied logic.

"What kind of client?" he asked.

"Once you meet the man, you'll understand why I couldn't turn him down."

"Damn right," Chester added, exchanging his cigar for a peppermint when the bailiff scowled at him. "The moment I saw that tortured face of his I dug out a jug and offered him a drink. How was I to know he'd turn out to be a temple Mormon?"

"No you don't," Traveler said. "You're not taking me in." He knew that Barney would never offer alcohol to anyone who might be offended. Certainly not to a Mormon in good enough standing to have temple access.

"Besides which," Martin went on, "this case will get you out of town, Moroni. It will be like a vacation."

"What kind of case?" Traveler repeated.

"'Evil is stalking the land,'" Bill responded. He rattled his newspaper to show he was quoting a reliable source. "That's the word from none other than Elton Woolley himself, the living prophet of Mormonism. He says the fires in the mountains are proof that God and the devil are fighting one another for our souls."

"There's a drought going on, for God's sake," Martin said. "The mountains are like tinder."

"The devil's work," Bill added.

"I thought God made the rain," Chester said.

Having heard it all before, Traveler shook his head and got up to stretch. Claire did the same, fanning herself with a magazine, creating a breeze that engulfed him in her rosewater perfume. The last time he'd smelled it he'd broken a man's leg and gotten himself charged with assault.

His eyes were about to wander in her direction again

when the jury began filing back into the box. A moment later, the judge took his seat and Prosecutor Young, whose name was as common as Smith in a state teeming with the ancestors of Brigham Young's polygamous efforts, began his final argument.

"Don't be fooled by the man you see sitting before you, ladies and gentlemen of the jury. Though charged with simple assault, assault with a deadly weapon would be more appropriate. He's a professional, a private detective, a former linebacker for the Los Angeles football team. Look at him. The defendant is six feet three inches tall and weighs more than two hundred and twenty pounds. He's a weapon in himself."

The prosecutor paused to stare Traveler in the face. "The defense will tell you that he had no choice, that it was self-defense. That it was three against one. But just let me tell you what the *Los Angeles Times* had to say about him." With a dramatic gesture, he picked up a clipping from the prosecutor's table.

"Objection," Critchlow said quietly, without emotion. "That's hearsay."

"Sustained," the judge said.

But Traveler's memory wasn't so easily edited. *Moroni Traveler plays linebacker like a rabid dog,* the newspaper had said.

"Imagine yourselves under attack by this man," the prosecutor continued.

Traveler looked at the jurors. He hoped it wasn't fear he saw on their faces.

"You've heard from Claire Bennion, the woman he once lived with." Young smiled at her. "A woman who wanted only reconciliation but ended up having to defend herself against this man's vicious attack."

Traveler sighed. She'd been the one to attack first, and on the telephone like so many times before. Sucking him in at two in the morning despite his previous pledge to Martin to stop playing her crazy games.

"*Moroni, it's about your son. I . . . he needs your help.*"

"*I have no son.*"

"*I named him after you.*"

"*We've been over this before, Claire.*"

"*Moroni Traveler the Third.*"

"*It was my father you named in the paternity suit.*"

"*You know better. I was thinking about you at the moment of conception.*"

"*That doesn't make him a Traveler.*"

"*Why did you and your father offer to adopt him then?*"

Traveler wasn't about to explain, not to a woman like Claire. How could he tell her that the boy would have been as much a son to him as Traveler had been to Martin? A matter of upbringing instead of genes.

The prosecutor, looming in front of the defendant's table, pointed a finger at Traveler. "Miss Bennion asked some friends over to meet Mr. Traveler, her lover, the man she wanted to marry. She was going to cook dinner, make a party of it. Instead, one of her guests ended up in the hospital."

"*They've taken your son away from me,*" Claire had said.

"*Who has?*"

"*That's why I need your help.*"

"*We've been through this kind of thing before, Claire.*"

"*That was me then. Now we're talking about your son, your namesake.*"

"*You're lying.*"

"*Are you sure?*"

"*All right. Tell me about it.*"

Her voice went soft, sexual. "*I'm afraid. It's dangerous to stay on the phone. I'll tell you everything when you get here.*"

"*You've done this before, Claire.*" *He'd lost count of how many times it was now.*

"You always come to my rescue." She gave him an address on Third Avenue near E Street.

"You've moved."

"I had to." Her voice caught, the way it always had at the point of entry when they were making love. *"Oh, God. Come to me. Now."*

The prosecutor shook his head. "The defendant said he had no choice. But I say there's always a choice when it comes to breaking a man's leg the way he did."

They were waiting for Traveler in an otherwise empty apartment. The four of them. Claire and three big men who looked to be about ten years out of high school and probably that far out of shape. They'd all been drinking, but not enough to keep them from recognizing Traveler.

"Jesus Christ. He's the one who killed that running back."

"Crippled him, you mean."

"What the fuck's the difference? The gamoosh ended up a turnip."

"That was one on one. There's three of us."

"To hell with the odds."

"The winner gets me," Claire said, licking her lips to make absolutely certain they understood her meaning.

"And my son?" Traveler asked.

She laughed.

"Why are you doing this, Claire?"

"You're the detective."

"I should have known better."

"You're the Angel Moroni."

They came at him then. Which gave him no choice. He had to put one of them out of the game immediately. Breaking bone was the quickest way. The sound of it, the snap and the scream, took the fight out of the other two.

That broken bone was on display twenty feet away, complete with autographed cast. Claire's name was signed in red inside a lipstick heart. *To Clint with love.*

She used to draw the same kind of hearts on Traveler when they were in bed. Sometimes she'd lick them off, depending on their location.

Had she done that with Clint? he wondered. Probably not. Claire wasn't the kind to pay in advance.

When Critchlow's turn came, he concentrated on Traveler's three attackers. Hired thugs, he called them. Two with police records. He didn't quite say Claire had hired them, but that was the implication.

When the jury came back an hour later, they looked Traveler in the eye, a good sign that Critchlow had prophesied in advance, and declared him not guilty.

Martin whooped like an Indian and rushed forward to hug his son, something he seldom did in public because of the difference in their heights. Once they broke apart, Barney Chester took a turn at squeezing Traveler, while Mad Bill kissed him on both cheeks. Charlie settled for a handshake, an emotional outburst for him.

Traveler was turning to Critchlow when he felt a tap on his shoulder. He swung around to see Willis Tanner's lopsided squint.

"None of this was necessary, Mo," Tanner said. His squint dissolved into a wink. "You know that."

Tanner was accompanied by Anson Horne, the cop who'd pretended to believe Claire's story. As the police chief's liaison officer with the church, he'd forced the city attorney to seek an indictment.

"This isn't the end of it," Horne said. "I—"

Tanner, as personal aide to the prophet, Elton Woolley, silenced the cop with a look.

Tanner patted Traveler on the back. "All you had to do was come to me, ask for my help, and none of this would have happened."

"Your price would have been too high," Traveler said.

Tanner feigned surprise. "I've never asked for a thing."

"I know you, Willis."

"How long have we been friends now, Mo. Since junior high school, isn't it?"

In Utah there are friends and there are Gentiles, Traveler reminded himself. The latter seldom qualified as more than acquaintances, since the Saints, as Mormons called themselves, had little time to waste on nonbelievers who were to be denied salvation anyway.

"Almost thirty years," Traveler said.

"In all that time have I ever traded on our friendship?"

"You weren't always working for the prophet."

"What does that mean?"

"That owing you would be like owing the church."

"We want your soul, Moroni, not your money."

"I don't like the sound of that," Martin said. "The Saints always want their ten percent."

"They tithe on your gross," Bill reminded. "Not your net. To prove yourself worthy of temple entry, you have to produce your 1040s."

Tanner's squint came back. "You Travelers are named for our angel. I've taken that as a sign since the day I met you." His gaze settled on Traveler's father, who'd exchanged the name Moroni for Martin the day he entered first grade. "I pray for the day of your return to us."

"Why are you here, Willis?" Traveler said.

"As a reminder that I'm always available to help."

Martin snapped his fingers. "Dammit, Mo. That reminds me. We've got a client waiting for your help."

He pulled his son toward the courtroom door.

Clint intercepted them, barring their way with an out-thrust crutch.

"Claire gave me this for you," he said, handing Traveler a note.

He hobbled away while Traveler read it. *The ways of the Lord and his angel Moroni are mysterious. So are mine.*

He tried to find her in the crowd, but she was nowhere to be seen.

A West Temple wino, two blocks east of his normal beat, was waiting for them on State Street. His baseball-capped head bobbed like one of those dashboard dolls as he loped along inside Mad Bill's sandwich board. Today's proclamation, posted on both sides in newsprint, declared THE FIRES OF HELL AWAIT.

Bill exchanged places with the man, who hurried away the moment Charlie paid him off with a bottle, a half pint judging by the size of its brown bag.

Bill spread his arms and took a deep, dramatic breath. "Smell that. Manna from heaven."

Charlie pointed toward the Wasatch Mountains. "Smoke signals from God."

Traveler followed the Indian's finger. Usually, the mountains were a constant reminder of Mormon efficiency. Of how they'd crossed that ten-thousand-foot barrier on foot and in covered wagons to find their promised land. Which turned out to be a desert sinkhole no one else wanted. Only Brigham Young knew better, knew that the mountains were high enough to hold snow the year round and thereby keep the creeks and rivers flowing in the hottest of summers.

Today, however, the mountains were a blur, obscured by smoke from the fires on the east bench.

"I feel like walking," Traveler said. The office was five blocks away, uphill all the way to South Temple Street.

"You've got a client waiting," Martin reminded him. "He's been there for hours."

"Don't worry about him," Barney Chester said, unwrapping a fresh cigar. "I left him plenty of magazines to read, *Improvement Era* and *Church News.*"

Both were Mormon periodicals that Barney kept stocked in magazine racks behind his cigar counter. He claimed they sold better than *Playboy.*

"Besides, I told him we wouldn't be back for hours."

"Then we'll walk," Martin said, "as long as we stop by the bank on the way."

"A wise precaution," Chester added, speaking around his cigar, his voice a bad imitation of Edward G. Robinson, whom he thought he resembled. "That way Bill and Charlie can act as guards."

They began walking north, Traveler and Martin in the lead, with Barney right behind them. Bill and Charlie held back a few yards, so they'd be free to solicit donations along the way. Panhandling, the police had called it on occasion. Bill preferred to think of it as tithing for his and Charlie's two-man religion, the Church of the True Prophet.

"Why do we need guards?" Traveler asked after one of Brigham Young's blocks, seven to a mile.

"Because of all the cash," his father answered. "The bail money."

"I thought you said we wouldn't need it."

Martin spread his hands, a gesture of innocence, while his face pleaded guilty.

"How much?"

"Not much. After all, Critchlow said the worst that could happen was probation."

"Dad?"

"We figured you might need getaway money," Chester said.

"Bribes," Bill called.

"Tithing," Charlie intoned.

Martin shook his head. "You turned down Willis Tanner's offer of help. That could have gotten you jail time, and a man my age doesn't want to be separated from his son. Even for a short time."

"Come on, out with it. How much cash are we talking about?"

Martin stopped at Third South. Zion's Bank was still four blocks away, three north and one west. He pulled a wad of bills the size of *The Book of Mormon* from his coat pocket. "I figured the bigger the war chest the better, so I cleaned out our savings. Barney added another two thousand to the pot. I didn't have time to mortgage the house."

"You're talking ten thousand dollars, for God's sake." Traveler checked the area for suspicious-looking characters, but found no one the equal of Bill or Charlie.

"Enough to get us out of the country if we had to," Martin went on, stuffing the money back into his pocket where it made such a bulge Traveler wondered why he hadn't noticed it in the first place.

"Out of state would have been good enough," Traveler said. "They don't usually extradite for simple assault."

"The church has a long reach. I've heard it said that your friend Willis is a member of the Danites."

"Who told you that?"

"Willis, actually. He hinted at it anyway, when I saw him this morning."

"He's bluffing," Traveler said without conviction.

The Danites were said to have been disbanded years ago,

though no one believed it. Whatever their present-day duties, membership was a closely guarded secret. In the beginning, they'd been Joseph Smith's spiritual vigilantes, empowered by the church's concept of blood atonement to murder as a means of cleansing sinners' souls.

"Wait a minute," Traveler said. "Why were you and Willis together this morning?"

"Another precaution," his father said.

"What was his price?"

"Don't worry about it. We only had to pay up in the event of conviction."

Traveler started walking.

"Wait up," Bill shouted. He trotted forward, his sandwich board banging his shins at each step. When he caught up he said, "Charlie thinks you ought to get out of town for a while, Mo."

The Indian nodded, a more usual comment from him than speech.

"That's what I've been telling you all along," Martin said. "That's why I took an out-of-town case for you."

"If you knew I would be free to take the case, why did you withdraw the money?"

Martin looked away, but not before Traveler saw the mist in his eyes. Traveler draped an arm around his father and squeezed affectionately.

"For Christ's sake," Martin growled. "This is Salt Lake. People will think we're a bunch of fairies." He kept his distance all the way to the bank.

Nephi Bates and another man, presumably Traveler's client, stood in the center of the Chester Building's lobby, their heads craned back to admire the Depression-era frescoes on the ceiling. Brigham Young was up there, leading a handcart battalion. So was Jim Bridger, the first white man to see the Great Salt Lake and spill the beans about it.

When Bates's eyes came down to earth, his look of adoration gave way to instant disappointment.

"I was hoping for a conviction," he said.

Usually he confined his comments to religion, giving rise to Barney Chester's contention that his elevator operator was a temple spy from across the street.

"We're sorry to disappoint you," Martin said.

"My prayers have been answered just the same."

Traveler waited for an explanation. When none came he looked to his father, who shrugged and said, "This is our client, Ellis Nibley."

From a distance Nibley had looked to be in his early forties. Up close he had the face of a sick old man, bone thin, with ashen skin and wrinkles like streaks of pain. Martin had been right about him. He'd be hard to turn down.

"Brother Nibley is just back from a baptism for the dead," Bates said.

"That's one of the reasons I'm here in Salt Lake," Nibley said.

Traveler wasn't about to ask about the other reasons in the lobby. "Would you please run us upstairs, Nephi?"

The elevator operator bit his lips before stepping to his gilt cage. Traveler gestured Nibley inside. The others knew enough to stay behind at Barney's cigar stand.

Traveler's office was on the third and top floor. One window looked north, toward the temple, the other east to the Wasatch Mountains. Both windows had been left open to catch a cross-breeze. But the rising heat of October's Indian summer was too much for the Chester Building, which had been built long before air conditioning.

Traveler shed his coat and tie and suggested that Nibley do the same. Nibley's only reply was to brush absently at his sleeves. His suit—Traveler pegged it for Sears or Montgomery Ward—still had store creases.

"You're not what I expected," he said.

Smiling, Traveler slipped behind the desk, his back to the temple window. His client sat down with a sigh, squinting against the light coming over Traveler's shoulder.

"You said something about coming here for a baptism," Traveler prompted.

"My wife's."

"Wasn't she a member of the church?"

"She was temple eligible all her life until the end. After what happened, I couldn't take the chance she wouldn't join me when I passed on."

Such baptisms were usually conducted for long-gone relatives who'd been born prior to Joe Smith's revelation on the subject of salvation.

"She strayed at the end," Nibley went on. "So I had to offer her the chance to rise."

She could turn it down, of course, which Martin promised to do if anyone tried raising him.

"Just what is it you want from me?" Traveler said.

Nibley's eyes widened as if suddenly adjusting to the light. "This city's too big for me. I feel lost the moment I arrive. The only reason I ever come here is to visit Brigham Young's temple. Here is where it started, so here is where I come to restore my faith."

His gaze shifted. From the look on his face, Traveler knew the man had focused on the temple spire across the street, probably on the golden statue of the Angel Moroni.

A gust of wind, crossing from one window to the other, played a note that might have come from Moroni's trumpet. At the sound Nibley shuddered. He shook his head hard to get his eyes back on Traveler.

"And did you restore yourself?" Traveler asked.

He bowed his head. "I never knew myself before . . . before Melba, my wife, passed on. I lived my life from one day to the other, never thinking ahead, never questioning my life. I accepted things as they were. I took them at face value." His head came up. "I thought life was perfect in Wasatch, that we were good people, blessed by God."

Traveler blinked. Wasatch was one of several small towns clustered in the middle of Sanpete County at the center of the state. A small county as population goes. Claire came from Sanpete.

Traveler got up and crossed the room to his father's desk. Half a dozen case folders, representing investigations still pending, littered the glass top. Not a bad case load for a man who claimed to be retired. The only thing Traveler had pending was Ellis Nibley.

Traveler pushed the folders aside to study the map of Utah that was under the glass. The cluster of towns at Sanpete's hub included Fairview, Mount Pleasant, Moroni, Spring City, Ephraim, Manti, and Wasatch. Adding them all together, the population couldn't have been more than ten thousand.

Moroni, Claire's hometown, looked to be no more than twenty miles from Wasatch.

Born in Moroni, she used to say, *raised in Moroni, and screwed by Moroni.*

Traveler swung around quickly, hoping to catch Nibley with a guilty look, something that might give him away as another of Claire's ruses. But Nibley had moved to the window, his face pressed against the pane.

"Does the name Claire Bennion mean anything to you?" Traveler asked the man's back.

No giveaway twitch, nothing, just a shake of his head as he backed away from the glass.

Traveler waited until Nibley settled back into the client's chair before continuing. "She comes from your part of the state."

"In my business—I own Nibley's General Store by the way—names are important. You greet a man by name when he comes into your place, chances are he'll be back."

He paused to run a forefinger among the fleshy folds of his ear. "Take the name Bennion, now. Claire doesn't come to mind. But I do remember a family of Bennions living over Moroni way."

"That's got to be them."

"The Bennions I'm thinking of could trace their stock back to one of the handcart battalions. Duane and Naomi Bennion, if I'm not mistaken."

"I wouldn't know about that."

"A big family." Nibley massaged an earlobe. "Sensible people when it came to having children. I remember my wife saying that. The Bennion boys arrived first, then the girls. Big brothers to look after them, that's what Melba said."

Nibley's hand dropped from his ear and landed in his lap, where it folded fingers with its mate. "The whole bunch of them, six or seven at least, used to come into the store whenever they visited Wasatch for a movie or to shop."

He sighed and closed his eyes. "I can see them now, Duane treating everybody to sodas and Popsicles."

"Tell me about the girls."

Nibley's eyeballs moved rapidly behind their lids. "Three of them, I think there were. Towheaded. Melba used to scoop them up, one after the other, and give them free peppermints. They reminded her of our daughter, Louise."

"The Claire Bennion I'm talking about is thin with black hair," Traveler said. "She's not someone you'd forget."

"They stopped coming about the time Moroni got its own general store. Though I seem to remember hearing that the family moved away about the time their youngest girl entered high school." He opened his eyes and nodded. "Her name was Kit if I'm not mistaken, not Claire. Why do you ask, anyway?"

Traveler glared at him, hoping for some telltale sign of guilt. "Let's get back to you, Mr. Nibley. You still haven't told me your problem."

Nibley took a deep breath. "It's not easy talking to a stranger."

Suddenly Traveler felt ashamed of himself. One look should have told him that Ellis Nibley wasn't Claire's type of co-conspirator. His was the same tortured face Traveler had seen in his own mirror often enough.

"I lied to you before," Nibley said. "My real reason for coming to Salt Lake was to hire a private detective. I'd planned on picking one out of the phone book, but then I read about you in the newspaper. About how you took on three men and won."

"That had nothing to do with business," Traveler said.

"I admire a man who doesn't back off."

"Sometimes that's the smartest thing to do."

Nibley tilted his head to one side as if trying to get a look at Traveler from another angle. "I was married to my wife for nearly thirty years, Mr. Traveler. That's why I have to know why she killed herself."

Traveler swiveled his chair around until he was looking at the temple. "That's the kind of question best answered across the street."

"You'd think a husband would know his wife better than anyone, wouldn't you? God knows I thought I did. If I was wrong about that, I could be wrong about anything."

Nibley's reflection pointed at the temple.

"Was she ill?" Traveler said.

"I checked with Doctor Joe's nurse. She said Melba passed her annual physical with flying colors."

Deliberately, Traveler kept his back to the man. "How were things between you and your wife?"

"Some personal problems cropped up recently. But nothing important, not after living together for thirty years. At least . . . Hell, I don't know anymore."

Judging from the way he said it, the problems were probably sexual. Menopause perhaps, male or female.

Traveler swiveled just enough to better his angle at Nibley's reflection. Glare off the Angel Moroni blurred the man's expression but not the fact that he was rubbing his face with both hands. The movement produced a scratching sound, either rough skin or whiskers, Traveler couldn't tell which without turning around. Yet Nibley's sigh was clear enough. It was a sound of surrender.

"We hadn't slept together in a long time, what with Melba going through the change and all. She made it without a hitch though. Doctor Joe said so himself. I'll tell you, that man was a healer, a saint, a . . ."

He covered his face again in a vain attempt to muffle a sob.

Traveler spoke quickly. "Do you suspect something other than suicide?"

"Oh, no. She left me a note."

"What did she say?" Traveler asked softly.

"Only that she was sorry."

Traveler faced his client once again. "Take my advice, then. Leave it at that."

Nibley had eyes only for the Angel Moroni. "Melba worked in the store with me since the day I opened it. Now it feels empty, no matter how many customers I've got. You see"—he was aiming his words at the angel—"I never loved another woman, spiritually or physically. That's why Melba and I married in the temple, so we could be sealed together for time and all eternity."

Traveler recognized Mormon doctrine word for word. "I can't do you any good, Mr. Nibley. The one person who knows the truth is gone. Chances are you'd be wasting your money hiring me."

Nibley nodded, but the gesture didn't seem meant for Traveler.

"My wife cleaned the house before she killed herself, probably so the neighbors wouldn't see it messy. Then she put on her face—that's what she said every time she put on lipstick and mascara—before taking an entire bottle of pills."

"What kind?"

Nibley stood up and stepped around the desk to get closer to the window. He bowed his head as if he were listening to the angel. For a moment his lips moved in silent prayer. "They told me it was tranquilizers. I guess she got them from Doctor Joe, though I don't know why Melba needed such things."

"You didn't know about her medication?"

"Not a word. I don't believe in taking anything stronger than aspirin."

"Who's this Doctor Joe?"

"He's been our family physician for years." Nibley reached out slowly until his fingertips touched the glass. "Her suicide nearly killed my daughter. My sons blame me for what happened. They don't say so out loud, but I can see it in their faces."

"I still don't see how I can help," Traveler said.

Nibley twitched. His anguished eyes came away from the angel. "I came to you because I don't know what else to do. I've got to know why she did it."

"A happily married woman doesn't kill herself," Traveler said. "So chances are the only thing I'm going to find out is bad news."

"I don't care. I must know if I failed her."

Traveler shook his head slowly. Suicide was a no-win situation. Yet he couldn't bring himself to say no just yet. "When did she kill herself?"

"Six weeks ago."

"Why wait until now to come to me?"

"When someone else I know died recently, I suddenly began feeling as if all my ties were being cut. As if I no longer belonged anyplace. Can you understand that?"

Traveler had felt the same way a year or so back when he thought his father was dying of cancer.

"An investigation can be expensive," he said, since Nibley looked far from prosperous despite his new suit. Even the average Salt Lake salary—kept down by the church's constant importing of cheap laborers, also known as converts—would seem like a fortune to someone from a town as small as Wasatch. "My fee is three hundred dollars a day."

Calmly, his expression never changing, Nibley extracted a well-worn leather wallet from his back pocket. He held it out toward Traveler to show off the hand-tooled beehive, a traditional Mormon emblem. "Mel, my youngest son, made this for me in junior high shop."

He turned the wallet over. Another sacred Mormon symbol, the sea gull, had been etched on the other side. Once Traveler had nodded his appreciation of the workmanship, Nibley began counting out hundred-dollar bills. He didn't stop till he'd reached fifteen.

"That's five days, Mr. Traveler, a working week in advance."

Traveler made no move toward the bills now sitting on the edge of his desk.

"Mother and I saved all our lives," Nibley went on, keeping his eyes on the money. "We were planning on taking a late-life mission together. Now there's nothing worth saving for."

"You have children," Traveler reminded him.

"They've been taken care of, don't you worry. The house and the business go to them. This was our money, Mother's and mine. Mad money, she called it. Our getaway fund."

Traveler felt like getting away, too. But investigating a suicide in Wasatch was not what he had in mind. Still, he knew he was stuck. Martin had already committed him, signed and sealed. So he might as well start gathering the facts.

"What about your children, Mr. Nibley? Do they still live in Wasatch?"

"I know what they say about people like us living out in the sticks. How can you keep them down in Sanpete after they've seen Salt Lake?" He looked up from the money long enough to force a smile. "I brought up my kids right. They've stayed put. My daughter is Louise Dority."

His tone of voice said that ought to mean something, so Traveler nodded obligingly.

"Her husband, Clement Dority, owns one of the biggest

turkey farms around. Big enough to hire on both my boys, Mel and Ellis Junior, as hands."

Turkeys, Traveler seemed to recall, were a Sanpete staple.

"Take the money," Nibley said, pushing the bills at Traveler. "I don't want to look at it anymore. It reminds me that we waited too long to go on our mission, Mother and me."

Wishing his father had taken the case instead, Traveler opened a desk drawer and swept the money inside.

He was about to ask for details of the woman's death— time, place, who found her—when Nibley continued. "I feel better already, knowing you're going to help. Maybe now I can sleep without seeing Mother's face in that casket."

"I need some names," Traveler said, changing tactics, deciding not to rehash details that could be checked easily enough once he arrived in Wasatch. "Somewhere to start. Your wife's close friends, for instance."

"There's our neighbor, Shirley Colton. She and Melba were always together, swapping recipes and volunteering in the Relief Society."

Traveler wrote that down. "Anyone else?"

"Since you're here in Salt Lake, you might want to talk to my wife's cousin. Her name's Ann Ireson. She and Melba were very close growing up together in Wasatch. But we . . . I haven't seen the woman in years."

"Is there any special reason for that?" Traveler asked, suspecting the usual reason for such a separation, loss of faith in the church.

"She's one of those who don't like men, if you ask me." He looked away, but not before Traveler saw his uneasiness.

"Do you have an address?"

"She's in the phone book under her husband's name, Thomas Ireson."

Nothing ever changes, Traveler thought. The woman had probably married outside the church, condemning herself to hell as a Gentile to Nibley's way of thinking.

Traveler got up and came around the desk. "I'll contact you in Wasatch if I need anything else."

"How soon will I hear from you?"

"I'll leave first thing tomorrow morning."

Nibley nodded and stood up. He offered a leathery hand for shaking. "Thank you again, Mr. Traveler."

"Don't expect miracles."

"From a man named for an angel?" He smiled and went to the door. "About that woman you mentioned. Now that I think about it, I believe the youngest Bennion girl *was* named Claire. Kit was only her nickname."

Moments after Nibley left the office, Martin returned.

"Well, are you taking the case?" he asked as soon as the door closed behind him.

"Have you forgotten what you told me about suicides?"

"Never quote me to my face."

"'They're no-win situations,' you said, 'like working for the church. Stay away from both of them like the plague.'"

"My God. How could you turn that man down?"

"'Don't get personally involved.' I believe that's another of your ten commandments for survival. It comes right after 'Don't be ruled by emotion.'"

"Did you look into that man's eyes?" Martin asked.

Traveler nodded. "Did we see the same thing?"

"Losing his wife was like losing his faith," Martin said, sagging into his desk chair. "That's what I saw." He let out a deep, weary breath. "Look at me. What do you see?"

Exhaustion, Traveler thought. Wrinkles that hadn't been

there before the trial. "Relax, Dad. You know me. I'm leaving for Wasatch first thing in the morning."

Martin swiveled away to hide his emotions just as Traveler had done with Nibley.

"The pigeons are after him today," Martin said with a nod toward the street.

Traveler knew he was referring to the statue of Brigham Young that stood at the head of Main where it ran into South Temple Street.

"Piss-poor prior planning," Martin said. "The man's still got his back to the temple and his hand out to the bank."

"The bank wasn't there when they put up the statue."

Martin swung around wearing a smile that added new wrinkles while erasing others. "How much did you charge Ellis Nibley?"

"The usual. Three hundred a day."

Martin held out his hand. Traveler shrugged, retrieved Nibley's money from the desk, and surrendered it.

"I'll send him a refund tomorrow," Martin said.

"How much?"

"Going to Sanpete County's as good as a vacation. I told you that before."

"Maybe I should pay him."

"A hundred per diem ought to do it if you don't make a federal case out of this."

"And expenses?"

"You're no businessman, Moroni. If it weren't for my missing persons cases"—Martin paused, his smile broader than ever, to tap the stack of file folders on his desk—"we wouldn't make the rent."

"Speaking of which, Dad, I want you to find the boy for me while I'm away in Wasatch."

The smile faded. "That's a lost cause. Claire never meant us to have him."

"All I'm asking is that you find him. I'll do the rest."

"Let it go, Moroni."

"Either you do it while I'm gone or I'll have to do it myself when I get back."

"We don't know for sure if she ever had the child. The whole thing could have been a scam. Maybe she was never pregnant."

"She disappeared long enough to have a child."

"Claire has been disappearing ever since you've known her."

"Not for nine months."

"Sometimes I think it would be better if gestation time varied depending on the woman."

Traveler held his breath, wondering if the subject of his own birth was about to come up. A birth that had taken place more than a year after Martin went away to war.

"Have you thought this through?" Martin said.

"I have to know about the boy."

"We may never know for sure. Sometimes they can't be found."

"There can't be that many Moroni Traveler the Thirds around."

"I used to say the same thing about Kary, your mother. That there couldn't be too many women like her around. But you found Claire, didn't you?"

"You make it sound like it was deliberate," Traveler said.

"Let me tell you about your mother. She always had a new set of friends, from the time I met her until the day she died. Women friends, not men. Invariably she'd introduce each one to me as her best and dearest friend. But if I happened to mention her a week later, it was as if your mother had never heard the name before. She changed friends like the rest of us change clothes."

"Maybe she was jealous that you remembered another woman's name."

"You were at the funeral. She had no friends. Nobody came but us."

Did you love her? Traveler wanted to ask, but knew he never would. Probably Martin wanted to ask the same kind of question of him.

"Will you look for the boy?" Traveler asked.

"Tell me one thing. Do you still want to adopt him or is it Claire you're after?"

"You know me better than that."

"Do I?"

Ann Ireson, the dead woman's cousin and childhood friend, lived in Holladay, a rural suburb south of town. It was the second place settled by the Mormons after their arrival and was part of Brigham Young's master plan to expand his empire by securing his borders with armies of the faithful. Before he died, those borders extended all the way into Idaho, Nevada, Arizona, and California.

The Ireson house was one of those grim Tudor cottages that sprung up during the Depression. It had all the right ingredients—an exposed chimney, clipped gables, and a rolled asphalt roof doing its best to imitate thatch. But everything had been built on too small a scale, as if diminished by hard times.

The woman who opened the door had been constructed on a far grander scale. The Valkyries came to mind.

She smiled at his wandering eyes. "Mr. Traveler?"

He nodded, wondering what it would be like to have her

carry him off to Valhalla. "I appreciate you seeing me on such short notice, Mrs. Ireson."

"My husband was against it. He thinks Melba broke faith by killing herself."

"And you?"

"I'm talking to you, aren't I? Now please come in."

He followed her into a ransacked living room.

"The grandchildren were here yesterday," she explained.

Surprise must have shown on his face. "I married when I was very young, Mr. Traveler."

Mathematics and a dozen framed family photographs on a baby grand told him that her daughters must have followed in their mother's child-bride footsteps.

"Too young, I think sometimes," she added while restoring a cushion to an overstuffed chair so that he could sit down. "Now what is it you want to know about my cousin?"

"I need to start somewhere, so whatever you can tell me will be very helpful."

She fussed with a matching chair but remained standing behind it, seeming to use the chair's back as a barrier against him. "You have to understand. We were more than cousins. She was my first real friend. We shared everything, our childhood, our secrets, our hopes. And that damned town, too. We shared that."

She left the chair for the sofa, clearing away enough toys so that she had room to curl up facing him. Behind her, a picture window framed the Wasatch Mountains. "I'm only sorry that she didn't have the chance to escape from that town when I did."

"Why was that?"

"Ellis Nibley, of course."

When Traveler phoned earlier, he hadn't mentioned Nibley's name, only that he was concerned with the circumstances of Melba's death.

"Mr. Nibley is my client."

"That's what I thought. No doubt he hired you to soothe his conscience."

"About what?"

"My husband is an older man, Mr. Traveler. He was already in business for himself when I married him. Perhaps you've heard of Howard's Heavenly Pizza?"

Traveler nodded that he had.

"There was only the one small stand to start with. In Sugarhouse. I worked there myself until I got pregnant." The glint in her eye said that hadn't been long. "As soon as Howard expanded, I pestered him until he finally offered Ellis a job. It could have turned into a partnership. Ellis knew that, but he said Wasatch was where he was born and that's where he would die. The truth was, he inherited the general store from his father and didn't have the guts to try anything else. In any case, his decision condemned Melba. So as far as I'm concerned, he's more to blame for her suicide than she is."

"Why do you say that?"

"Let me tell you something about the town of Wasatch. Getting out of there saved my sanity."

She leaned back, gaining as much distance from him as the sofa allowed.

"When I was growing up," she said, "there were two thousand people in Wasatch. Now there's only fourteen hundred and it's still shrinking. That says something about the place, don't you think? That anybody who can gets out of there. The trouble is, too many have to die to do it."

She paused. Her eyes began to moisten. "Have you ever been there, Mr. Traveler? To Wasatch?"

"Only driving through."

"You had the right idea. It's not a place you'd want to stop. It's . . . oh, God."

She bent over at the waist as if suddenly stricken by a cramp. He started to get up to help but she waved him back. Sobs shook her shoulders.

Before he could offer his handkerchief, she pulled a wadded tissue from the sleeve of her blouse and blew her nose.

"Damn," she said, sitting up. "I thought I'd finished crying."

"Could I get you a glass of water or something?"

She didn't seem to hear. "The people in Wasatch are living in the past. They think their religion is all the protection they need against evil. But God has turned his back on women in that town."

He assumed she was referring to the usual church dogma, that this was a man's world and so was heaven, that it was a husband's prerogative to raise his wife to kingdom come when the time came.

"Look," she said, struggling to her feet to point toward the picture window behind her. "I live in the shadow of the Wasatch Mountains. Their name is a constant reminder of the town where I was born. Of what it was like for me, a woman, growing up there. For what it was like for Melba."

Traveler got up to stand beside her, to stare at the ten-thousand-foot barrier that had protected Brigham Young from his eastern enemies and given him the time to create a theocracy.

She hugged herself. "I assume you're going to Wasatch, Mr. Traveler?"

"As soon as I leave here."

"It's a man's world down there. Remember that and thank God you're not a woman."

HENRY THE EIGHTH
PRINCE OF FRISKERS
LOST FIVE WIVES
BUT KEPT
HIS WHISKERS
BURMA-SHAVE

Traveler was a hundred and ten miles out of Salt Lake City on U.S. 89, well into Sanpete County, when the last of the signs flashed by. All six of them, as bleached and threadbare as old bone, were still readable.

The marker for the Moroni turnoff hadn't fared as well. It was full of holes and hanging precariously on posts eaten away by deer hunters getting a jump on the season.

He pulled onto the shoulder to study his road map, running his finger along 89's narrow red line. Apparently he was already within the city limits of Mount Pleasant, though the

only sign of habitation was an abandoned service station that
looked like it had been left over from the Depression. After
Mount Pleasant came Spring City, Wasatch, Ephraim, and
Manti.

Claire's hometown, Moroni, was eight miles west, at the
end of a thin black line labeled State Highway 116. He
could be there in ten or fifteen minutes, looking for clues to
where she'd hidden the boy. Or perhaps even a clue to
Claire herself.

Traveler shook his head and refolded the road map.
Whatever clues Claire had left behind could wait a while
longer.

Another message was waiting for him outside Wasatch.

> DOES YOUR HUSBAND
> MISBEHAVE
> GRUNT AND GRUMBLE
> RANT AND RAVE
> SHOOT THE BRUTE SOME
> BURMA-SHAVE

Wasatch was a cul-de-sac at the end of a mile-long side
road that terminated against the foothills. It had been settled twice, Traveler recalled from his father's briefing,
once by Brigham Young's pioneers and again after Utah's
Indian wars. A city-limits sign gave the town's population
as 1,324.

Traveler rolled down the window, expecting the air to be
cold from the snow-capped peaks of the Wasatch Plateau.
Instead, the noontime air was hot enough to smell scorched.

The thought crossed his mind that he'd carried the forest
fires south with him. But there was no sign of smoke, only
blue sky and mountains. Probably he'd been smelling smoke
all along and hadn't noticed it. No doubt the scent was

clinging to his jeans or to the red flannel shirt that Martin had insisted on since deer hunting season was about to start.

Rows of columnlike poplar trees followed him along Main Street. So did nineteenth-century barns, hay derricks, and outhouses. When they gave out, irrigation ditches and sluice gates continued all the way to Brigham Street, where sidewalks and gutters marked the beginning of the business section.

A block beyond Brigham, at Kimball Street, he found the city hall. It was a square, two-story building with a flat roof and a limestone facade accentuated by rock-faced lintels, sills, and arched windows with projecting keystones. It also served as a fire station. No doubt Martin would have called it a fine example of the Victorian Revival style. Utah Gothic came to mind as Traveler climbed the outside wooden stairway to the sheriff's office.

A weathered sign, hand lettered in black going on gray, hung from the lintel above the open door. It read MAHONRI HICKMAN, SHERIFF.

Traveler knocked on the doorframe before entering. The room was small, with a single square window and a ceiling not much taller than Traveler. The walls were whitewashed, the planked floor deeply grooved and blackened by wear. A single wooden desk, fronted by two metal folding chairs, blocked the way to a squat doorway that probably led to a cell. A gunbelt hung on a peg beside the door.

The man sitting behind the desk stood up. He was small and wiry, about eighty pounds short of Traveler's two hundred and twenty. He wore jeans and a light blue uniform shirt with navy blue collar tabs.

"I'm Sheriff Hickman. You must be the private detective."

Small-town secrets were hard to keep, Traveler thought, handing over a photostat of his investigator's license. Even so, he hadn't expected instant recognition, especially when it came to something as sensitive as suicide.

The sheriff studied the photostat carefully, comparing the photo with real life. What hair Hickman had was concentrated in long, bushy sideburns that connected to an extravagant black mustache. He reminded Traveler of the faces in pioneer daguerreotypes.

He returned the ID and shook hands. "We've never had a private eye in Wasatch before. Not to my knowledge anyway. You being here puts us on the map, I guess. Sit down. We'd better talk before you start stirring up things around here."

The metal chair groaned under Traveler's weight.

"Let me tell you something about small towns," Hickman said, smiling as if he'd already read Traveler's mind on the subject. "I've lived my entire life in them. I was born in Manti myself, the best of the bunch as far as I'm concerned. While the rest of these towns shrink away to nothing, Manti endures. Of course, it's a temple town. Brigham Young himself dedicated the temple site. As far as I'm concerned that makes Manti the capital of Sanpete County."

The sheriff sat back, staring at Traveler over steepled fingers as if daring a challenge.

"I seem to remember that Ephraim's the largest town," Traveler said.

"Let me tell you about Ephraim. They don't call it Little Denmark for nothing. Those people are still living like they did in the old country, backsliders who are too fond of their pipes and coffee and barley beer. Ignore the Word of Wisdom like that and God knows what comes next."

"How did you end up in Wasatch?" Traveler asked, though what he really wanted to know was how the sheriff knew he was coming.

"I have one goal in life, Traveler, to be the sheriff of Manti. This is a first step only."

The faded sign over the door had been there a long time, Traveler thought but didn't say so. Hickman looked to be forty-five, maybe more. He'd have to hurry his career if he was going anywhere before retirement.

"Does the name Hickman mean anything to you?"

Traveler sat back, recognizing the question as rhetorical. He also recognized the name.

"Bill Hickman, the defender of the faith, was my great-grandfather."

In the beginning, Traveler knew, Hickman had been one of Joseph Smith's twelve bodyguards.

"Brigham Young personally rewarded Bill by appointing him a sheriff."

He was also known as Brigham's Destroying Angel, claiming to have committed murder in the name of the prophet.

"Bill was a saint."

Brigham Young excommunicated him in the end.

"Mahonri Hickman will be a name to be reckoned with one day, too." The sheriff leaned forward to solicit a response.

"Who told you I was coming?" Traveler said.

"Running you out of town might be a step in the right direction, considering the publicity it ought to generate." The sheriff smiled and fingered his mustache like a cliché villain. "I figured someone like you'd be coming around when Ellis Nibley paid me a visit. Sat in the same chair you are not three days ago and asked my advice about hiring himself a big-city detective. He wouldn't listen to me. I don't suppose you will either?"

"I haven't heard your advice yet."

Hickman stood up and strapped on his gun, a .357 Magnum. "You're a foot taller than I am, big man. But that doesn't mean shit if push comes to shove. I want you to know that if the time arrives when I have to put you in your place."

Hickman dropped back into his seat and stared Traveler

in the eye. "We're country folk around here. We go to
church, pay our tithe, and mind our own business. That
means we don't go around asking questions about the dead.
On top of which, you're on a fool's errand."

"It won't be my first."

Hickman scowled. "The only crime committed was by
Melba Nibley. A crime against God. So my advice to you is
to get back in your car and go home."

"Is that an order?"

The sheriff pulled the tip of his mustache hard enough to
create a crooked smile. "As my illustrious ancestor always
said, 'It's a free country.' Free to be buried in."

"Is that a threat?"

"All I'm saying is I don't want you upsetting folks."

"I suppose everyone in town already knows why I'm
here?"

"Not unless Nibley told them."

"Look, I'm here to help the man if I can."

"How much do they pay you for that kind of work?"

"Not enough," Traveler said, thinking of the refund his
father had insisted upon.

Hickman sighed. "Yeah, I know what you mean. Maybe I
came on too strong there for a minute. But this thing's
damned near killed Ellis. Hell, maybe you being here will
clear the air for him. I don't know. I tried my best to help,
but I couldn't get through to him."

"Tell me about the suicide," Traveler said, "and I won't
have to bother anybody else for the details."

Hickman chewed on his mustache for a moment. "Judging from what I read, women like to use pills. It's not so
messy." He squinted at Traveler as if waiting for an argument. "Melba must have been saving them up, because Doctor Joe would never prescribe enough drugs to kill anybody.
A great doctor as far as I'm concerned. Saving people was his
life, so he sure as hell wouldn't help them die."

"What kind of pills?" Traveler asked.

"I don't remember the technical name, but they were some kind of tranquilizer."

"Did you see her suicide coming?"

"Melba Nibley was a good woman. She taught Sunday school. She was past president of the church's Relief Society."

"Do you have any doubt that it was suicide?"

"Come on. She left a note."

"In her own hand?"

"You're damn right. I've had it verified too."

"Do you have any idea why she might have done it?" Traveler asked.

"If Ellis Nibley doesn't know, who would?"

To give himself time to think, Traveler got up and stepped to the window. His father would have loved the Beaux Arts theater across the street. It was another example of Victorian excess, complete with Corinthian columns, Roman statuary, scrollwork cornices, and parapets worthy of a medieval castle. Faded letters on its marquee said CLOSED FOR REPAIRS. The announcement looked as if it had been there for years.

He took a deep breath. He was wasting his time in Wasatch; he'd known that from the start. There was nothing he could do to ease Ellis Nibley's pain. Worse yet, Traveler's presence would probably inflame wounds not yet healed.

"Where did you find the body?"

"Dressed in her Sunday best lying in her own bathtub. A practical woman, Melba Nibley. She knew about bodily fluids."

"Is there anything else I ought to know?" Traveler asked, turning to face the sheriff again.

"Like what?"

Traveler waited, hoping silence would elicit something more. But Hickman pursed his lips inward so hard they disappeared inside his mustache.

"I'd like to talk to some local people," Traveler said finally. "To earn my keep."

"Don't I count?"

"I was thinking of Mrs. Nibley's friends."

"You won't find people home this time of day, not in Wasatch. The best time to catch folks is suppertime, right after sundown. Don't be late, though. We go to bed early around here."

Sheriff Hickman folded his arms over his chest. "It's Monday night, you know."

To Mormons, Monday nights were known as Family Home Evenings, traditionally a time to gather together for prayer and songs, though television had taken its toll.

"I'll try them at work," Traveler said. "Starting with Shirley Colton if you'd help me find her."

"She'll be at the post office. It's also our hardware store. It's just up Main Street, a coupla doors this side of Pratt Road. You can't miss it. The fact is, I'll give them a call and let them know you're coming."

"Advance warning is never a good idea in my business."

Hickman smiled. "Have you got a place to stay in town?"

"Not yet."

"I'll call the Beasleys at the Sleep-Well Motel."

"I passed the Uinta Hotel on Main Street. It looked okay."

Hickman dismissed the hotel with a wave of his hand. "When the word gets around that you're a detective—a Gentile at that, I figure—and that you're poking your nose into Melba Nibley's suicide, you'll have to drive all the way to Ephraim to get yourself a room. I wouldn't wish that on anybody."

"Where do I find the motel?"

"Go back down Main toward the highway. When you come to Cannon Street take a left. The Sleep-Well's a couple of blocks after that, right on Cowdery Creek. It's a nice spot."

Traveler started to leave.

"If you ask me," the sheriff called after him, "it's a waste of time you being here. Nobody in Wasatch is going to talk to someone like you."

"It's about time you got here," Shirley Colton said the moment Traveler introduced himself. She came out from behind a wall of post office pigeonholes and led him into a corner of the hardware store well away from the front door. "I just now overheard my husband on the phone with Sheriff Hickman. There was mention of some kind of investigator being here in town. That must be you."

She was a small woman with a pale face full of freckles about to make the transition to age spots. COLTON'S, stitched in dark brown script, ran across the breast pocket of her tan smock.

"Lord knows we've been waiting long enough for you to get around to us," she went on. "I guess we should thank God you got here at all."

Traveler smiled to cover his surprise but kept his mouth shut. In his business, silence was golden as long as other people wanted to talk.

"We can't speak here for long," she said softly. "Not in front of everybody." She glanced toward the rear of the hardware store, where a heavyset man in a matching smock was helping a lady customer and trying to watch Traveler at the same time. The place smelled of sawdust and glue. Its well-worn wooden floor had grooved paths down aisles that led to nail bins and racks of garden tools.

She raised her voice. "Lew, you man the cash register while I show our *guest* around town." She emphasized the word guest, probably for the customer's benefit. "We shouldn't be too long."

Before they could leave, another customer, a middle-aged man with dark crew-cut hair and rimless no-nonsense glasses, entered the store.

"Afternoon, Nat. May I help you?"

"I dropped in to get some nails."

"You don't mind if I wait on a customer, do you, Mr. Traveler? Now, Nat, what exactly do you need?"

The customer patted the pocket of his gray overalls as if searching for a sample. But he was watching Traveler out of the corner of his eye. "I'd better talk that over with your husband."

She sighed. "I've been working this place with him for fifteen years, Nat."

He smiled condescendingly and moved toward the back of the store.

"Men," she breathed, not for Traveler's benefit but her own.

Silently, Traveler followed her outside onto the sidewalk. Seen from there, Colton Hardware was one of those streamlined buildings from the thirties. Art Moderne it was called, if Traveler remembered correctly, with rounded corners, curved glass, and a flat roof that left all the vents and stovepipes exposed. Compared to its nineteenth-century surroundings, it could have been an alien spaceship.

She paused to look up and down Main. There weren't more than half a dozen people on the street. Four of them were loitering in front of the Main Street Dinette across the way.

"I suppose we could get a cup of *coffee.*" She accentuated "coffee" the same way she had "guest" to let him know that she followed WOW, the Word of Wisdom against the sin of caffeine.

"Not for me," he said. The dinette had a sign out front that said MOM'S HOME COOKING. His own mother's home cooking had run to parsnip pancakes saturated with Crisco.

Shirley Colton nodded and turned east on Main Street, toward the Wasatch Mountains. It was hot for so late in the afternoon, ninety at least. The air smelled faintly of scorched asphalt.

She didn't speak again until they'd reached the corner and turned left on Pratt Road. "It's been months since a bunch of us got together and wrote to the state board. We'd given you up for a lost cause."

She was mistaking him for someone else, he thought. That didn't stop him from prompting her with a nod. Her face, he realized, had reddened considerably since he'd first met her.

"If you ask me," she continued, "you coming around here now is too late. It's like locking the barn door after the cows have escaped."

He didn't know what she was getting at. But whatever it was, it had put her face into full blush.

The business district ended one block north of Main Street, where Ridgon Avenue crossed Pratt. Shirley Colton stopped at the intersection, looking carefully both ways, before crossing the road into the residential area. There wasn't a car moving anywhere.

Head down, she stepped off the curb brusquely and

walked staring at her feet, ignoring the neighborhood of Hoover bungalows.

"I don't understand," he ventured.

"Now that you're here, we won't stand for a whitewashing. You can be sure of that." She stopped walking to confront him. Her face was redder than ever, yet now she was looking him in the eye, with anger overcoming her shyness. "How many women have to pay the price before you people do something? How long before you stop protecting your own even when they're guilty?"

Careful, he reminded himself. Don't lie but don't give anything away either. "You've got to bear with me, ma'am. I was just brought into the case."

"Why now? Why not sooner, before someone had to die?"

She was glaring at him, hands on hips, demanding an answer.

"I'm sorry, Mrs. Colton. I can't comment on an investigation in progress."

She began walking again, catching him by surprise and forcing him to trot to catch up. He was sweating. She was hugging herself against some kind of inner chill.

A block later, they crossed Almon Avenue and the houses changed from one century to another, with single-story bungalows giving way to the taller Victorians.

She didn't speak again until they reached Heber Street. "If you try sweeping this under the rug, Mr. Traveler, you and your kind are going to find yourselves in trouble. Even at this late date, we're prepared to go as far as need be to get satisfaction." She turned away from him to point across the street. "Do you see that house?"

It was one of those small, two-story Victorians masquerading as a mansion, with a rock-faced facade that reminded him of a dungeon. Yellowed Venetian blinds screened the windows and gave the place an abandoned look.

"That's where it happened," she said.

He stared at her, trying to wait her out. Finally he said, "Are you talking about Melba Nibley?"

"For heaven's sake. What do you think this is all about? That's why I brought you here. That's the Nibley house across the street. Some of us thought, prayed, that her death might tip the scales and get some action."

"I understand it was suicide."

"I don't care what you call it. We buried her like a Saint, which she was. A saint and a martyr."

"Why do you say that, Mrs. Colton?"

"I don't see how can you ask that if you've read our letters?"

He took a quick breath. "Please, tell me why you think she killed herself."

She pursed her lips. "I should have known when I saw they sent a man. It's what we were afraid of all along. You're like all the rest. You're here to protect the interests of the medical board. How many women do you have on that board, Mr. Traveler? No, you don't have to answer. I can see the truth on your face."

He didn't know what she was seeing, bewilderment probably. "I'm only trying to do my job."

She stared at him for a moment but didn't speak until she was looking at the Nibley house. "Maybe you are. I don't know. Sometimes I think I don't know anything anymore."

She hugged herself again, so tightly her arms trembled. "Maybe God's the only one who knows why Melba did it. Unless her husband, Ellis, is lying to us."

"What are you suggesting?" Traveler said.

She backed up a couple of steps. "A woman owes respect and obedience to her husband. But if love gets in the way, the burden can become too heavy."

"I'm not sure what you mean, but that sounds very cynical to me."

"Not at all. I'm practical. You have to be to survive

nearly forty years of marriage like I have. But Melba. After thirty years with Ellis, she was still in love with him."

The thought crossed his mind that she might be playing games with him. That this conversation might have been cooked up by Sheriff Hickman to confuse a Gentile. Or maybe hurry him on his way out of town.

"Is there anything specific you can tell me about Melba Nibley's suicide?" he said.

"How can you ask that after reading our letters?"

"A good investigator has to keep an open mind at all times."

"Like I said before, Melba was a saint and martyr. Ask any woman in this town if you don't believe me. They'll all say the same thing. That he drove her to it."

"Who?"

"I hate to say it, but men are all the same. In the church or out. You think we're good for nothing more than sex."

Her eyes widened. She looked appalled by what she'd just said.

"I'm here to help," Traveler said.

She turned and fled back the way they'd come. He knew better than to chase a woman down the street in a town like Wasatch.

A block down from Colton's Hardware, sandwiched between Odell's Drugs and the Wasatch Co-Op, stood the
Uinta Hotel, a narrow red brick building, two rooms wide
and two stories high. It reminded Traveler of a firehouse.

The upstairs windows had their blinds drawn. The ones
on the ground floor were obscured by age and faded black
lettering: DAILY AND WEEKLY RATES on one side of the door,
HAROLD MCCONKIE, PROP. on the other.

Traveler hesitated outside the beveled-glass door. His reflection looked as faded as the hotel. He took a deep breath
of fresh air as a precaution against a stale lobby, and smelled
smoke. This time he saw its source, a column rising at the
head of Main Street where it dead-ended against the foothills
of the Wasatch Plateau. As far as he could tell the smoke was
coming from a heavily wooded area.

He hurried inside the hotel, intending to call the sheriff.
But Mahonri Hickman was in the lobby ahead of him, talking to the man behind the desk.

"You've got a fire in the hills," Traveler said.

"I already spotted it," the sheriff answered. "But thanks anyway."

"Where is it?" the clerk said.

"Looked to me like it's up near Ellsworth Flats."

"It could be a camp fire then."

"That's what I'm hoping," the sheriff said. "To be on the safe side, I'll drive up and take a look-see."

"You do that."

"I'm on my way then. I'll be in touch, Hal. With you, too, Traveler."

As soon as the sheriff left, Traveler took his place in front of the registration book. Its pages were as blank as the clerk's face. "I'd like a room, please."

The man shook his head. "I made a special trip over from the church offices to be here when you arrived."

"How'd you know I was coming?" Traveler asked, knowing the answer already.

"The sheriff makes it his business to keep me informed."

"You and who else?"

"My name's Harold McConkie. Bishop Harold Mc-Conkie. The sheriff said you'd be staying at the Sleep-Well Motel."

"I haven't checked in anywhere yet." Traveler stared into the man's bland face. A perfect bishop's face, Martin would have said. Unlined and worry-free. Confident and full of joy in its certainty of resurrection and everlasting life.

"We have no rooms available."

"I didn't know you had that many tourists here in Wasatch."

"I own the place. My wife runs it. There are only so many rooms she can keep open. Besides which, I'm also the volunteer fire chief. If that fire in the Wasatch turns into anything special, I won't have time to waste around here cleaning rooms."

Traveler smiled at the man, knowing damn well that a
Mormon male, particularly a bishop, wouldn't be cleaning
rooms in his own hotel.

"You'll like the Sleep-Well," McConkie added. "Nat
Beasley and his wife run a clean place."

"There's clean and there's clean," a woman said behind
him.

Traveler turned to see her descending the granite-treaded
staircase at the back of the lobby.

She clicked her tongue. "Sleep-Well indeed."

Before McConkie could answer, a siren went off, a series
of short, shrill blasts.

"Darn it," he said. "That was fast. Hickman must have
spotted something from the road. I've got to go, Eliza. You
look after things. By the way, this here is Mr. Traveler, the
investigator I told you about."

With that he hurried out of the hotel. The woman took
his place behind the desk.

"I was looking for a room right here in town," Traveler
told her, testing the waters.

"I'm Mrs. Bishop McConkie."

Like an army wife, she was letting him know the rank
she derived from her husband.

"I guess that means I don't get a room."

"Half the rooms here I keep for my children."

"How many do you have?"

"Bishop McConkie bought the Uinta for its ten-room ca-
pacity. But God didn't send us that many children."

"That leaves you room to spare, then."

"The bishop is very clear on that. When the siren goes,
he says there's always the chance that we might have to turn
the Uinta into a hospital, since we don't have one here in
town. Now, if you'll excuse me I'd better start getting things
ready."

"What about the beds at the Sleep-Well Motel?"

"Not up to hospital standards, I'm afraid. But they'd get the overflow from here if it came to that."

"You mean I might not have a room after all?"

"Nat Beasley is on the volunteer fire list, too, but only in the event of a second alarm. Even if that happens, his wife, Norma, can see to you."

"How do I get there?"

"Anyone can tell you. I have work to do."

The Sleep-Well Motel was at the west end of town on Cannon Street just beyond a WPA bridge that crossed Cowdery Creek. This late in the year the creek was nothing more than a series of stagnant pools.

Traveler parked out front and shook his head at the prospect before him, a half dozen clapboard cabins, all linked by sagging breezeways, all facing onto a pot-holed gravel driveway. Opposite the cabins was a shabby, flat-roofed shack that had once been a filling station. The faded printing was still readable on the molting stucco—ZION REST SERVICE. A hand-lettered plywood sign, OFFICE, hung from one of the abandoned gas pumps out front.

Swarming mosquitoes clouded around Traveler's head the moment he stepped from the car. He hurried into the office, but not fast enough to escape the smell of rotting vegetation coming from the creek bed.

"Shut the screen door after you, for heaven's sake," a

woman said without looking up from a telephone switch-board that had to be older than the motel. Behind the switchboard a metal door still had the original REST ROOM sign on it. "Where were you raised, in a barn?"

She, the switchboard, and an occupied playpen were crammed behind a pine lowboy that was serving as a counter. Traveler rested his elbows on the scarred top and leaned over to get a better look at the child. The boy blinked at him and made the kind of face that said tears were on the way. Traveler backed up a step.

"We've got enough bugs in here as it is. They're eating Baby Joe alive." She removed her headset, fussed with her dark hair for a moment, and then turned to face him. "You must be Mr. Traveler. I'm Norma Beasley. The sheriff called and told me to expect you. I hope it's hot enough for you."

He'd been expecting someone much older, someone to match the motel. But the woman in front of him couldn't have been more than thirty, about the same age as her flowered housedress if he was any judge. Sweat had pasted the thin material to her breasts and distended stomach.

"I've put you in our back cabin for privacy," she said. "It has the best view of the creek."

And the most mosquitoes, he thought. "What else did the sheriff have to say about me?"

She shrugged. "Mahonri Hickman isn't one to talk much."

"Not even to say that I'm an investigator?"

She turned away from him to bend over the playpen, but not before he'd seen the flash of recognition in her eyes. The redheaded boy stretched out his arms to be picked up. She obliged, hugging him to her breasts and kissing him to keep from looking at Traveler.

"How old is he?"

"Baby Joe's going on two," she said, still not meeting Traveler's eyes. "My husband is out back now, making up your room. I sent him on his way as soon as Mahonri called."

"The sheriff must have told you why I'm here."

"No," she said into the baby's ear.

Ask any woman in town, Traveler thought. That's what Shirley Colton had said. They'll tell you that Melba Nibley was a saint and a martyr.

"I've come about Mrs. Nibley."

That brought a stare, wide-eyed and fearful. After a moment, her head twitched as if she wanted to look away but couldn't control her muscles.

"How well did you know her?" he asked.

She wet her lips. "Shirley . . . Mrs. Colton said she forgot to check your credentials before she talked to you. That's something I won't do."

He showed her his license.

"You're not from the State Medical Board?"

That explained part of it, he thought. He'd been mistaken for a medical investigator. But the question was, why would they be expecting one in a town like Wasatch? The only thing that came to mind was Melba Nibley.

He said, "I didn't tell her I was from the state board."

"But Shirley understood . . ." Norma Beasley glanced through a grimy window that looked out onto the cabins. Beyond the cabins, thick smoke was now clearly visible in the foothills.

"I spoke with Mrs. Colton because I was told that she was a close friend of Melba's."

Mrs. Beasley stepped close enough to the window to touch it with her forehead. "Where is that man?"

When Baby Joe began crying, she dumped him in the playpen and went back to her switchboard to plug in a line. She used a regular phone this time instead of a headset. "Nat, he's here. I need you in the office right now."

Nathaniel Beasley was the same man Traveler had seen buying nails in Colton's Hardware. He'd changed out of his overalls and was wearing tan slacks and a short-sleeved

Hawaiian shirt that revealed arms so thin that sharp edges of bone showed through.

He ran skeletal fingers through his black, sweaty hair as he spoke. "I knew who you were right off." His voice was nasal, and as sharp as the rest of him.

"Did you find your nails?" Traveler asked.

"I had to put up the window screen in your room. Otherwise the mosquitoes would have sucked you dry in the night."

He peered out the window as if looking for insects. "This time of year you'd think we'd get a cool breeze off the mountains, wouldn't you? Come winter the wind off the Wasatch could freeze off your—"

"Watch your language in front of the baby," his wife interrupted.

". . . ears," he concluded. "That's all I was going to say, Norma. You know me."

"That's the trouble."

"Don't tell me about trouble. I've been watching the smoke. It's only a matter of time before they put out the second alarm."

"You've got no business being a volunteer, not with me and the baby to watch out for."

Beasley ignored her. "Do you know the country around here, Mr. Traveler?"

"I've driven Highway Eighty-nine before but never really stopped. I've hiked the Wasatch, too, but up around Salt Lake."

"Those are city mountains. Here it's so damned rugged we won't have a chance of stopping a fire if it really gets going in those canyons. Mark my words. We'll just have to let it burn itself out. Unless, of course, it heads for town. Then we'll have to make a stand."

He took a deep breath, expelling it noisily before grabbing a key from a hook on the wall next to the switchboard. "Come on. I'll show you your room."

"I'll bring fresh towels as soon as I change the baby," his wife said.

"I'll get them, Norma."

"No. That's my job. You go ahead."

Outside, the smell of smoke was as thick as the mosquitoes.

Beasley batted at the bugs absentmindedly. "There hasn't been lightning all summer. That means the fire's man-made. It has to be. I don't care what the bishop says."

"And what is that?" Traveler asks.

Beasley scratched a red, bug-bitten cheek. "It's no secret, I guess. He thinks it's spontaneous combustion, because nobody around here would be stupid enough to start a camp fire in this kind of weather. A stranger might, though." He squinted at Traveler.

"I just got here," Traveler reminded him.

"We're putting you in the end bungalow. Number six." Beasley started down the gravel drive toward the creek. The mosquitoes increased with every step. "Norma tells me you've been talking to Shirley Colton. She says you're here doing some kind of investigation. Is that right?"

"Everyone in town seems to know about it."

"Men your size don't usually like taking advice. But I'm offering it anyway. Don't believe everything you hear in this town. Especially from some of the women." He turned to look back at the office where his wife was watching them through the window. He raised his hand to her, more of a signal than a wave. "Some of them have gotten out of hand. My wife for one. Hysteria, I call it."

"She sounded all right when I talked to her."

"Thank God for that, eh?" Beasley said, still staring at her. He mouthed something that could have been *I love you.*

She raised one hand to her mouth, pretending to lock her lips like a child.

"Can you recommend someplace for dinner?" Traveler said.

"We've got two places in town. The Main Street Dinette and the Wasatch Cafe back on the highway." Beasley handed Traveler the key. "Make sure you lock yourself in at night." He snorted. "To keep out the bugs."

The Wasatch Cafe stood at the last bend of the highway before it turned into Main Street. Traveler pulled into the graveled parking area out front just as the sun disappeared behind the San Pitch Mountains to the west. Without competition, the neon Coors sign turned everything—clapboard siding, gravel parking lot, Traveler's skin—a jaundiced yellow.

He hesitated. There were a dozen cars there ahead of him, a big crowd for a place that couldn't have been more than thirty feet square. He couldn't count heads, though, because steam had blinded the front window.

Hunger started his stomach rumbling. His only alternative was the Main Street Dinette he'd seen while walking with Shirley Colton. Both places looked like worthy rivals to his mother's Crisco-coated cuisine.

What the hell. He had to have something, and a hamburger was a hamburger no matter where you got it.

Crossing the threshold, he tallied ten counter stools and standing room where the tables should have been. The standing room was filled, and so were the stools. Half the town's population seemed to be there, the male half. He was about to turn around and go looking for a grocery store when the counter emptied.

Refusing to be intimidated, Traveler climbed onto a center stool, still warm, and smiled at the waitress behind the counter. Her answering smile quivered around the edges.

The smell inside the steamy cafe reminded Traveler of Thanksgiving dinners from his childhood, when only the Jell-O mold was safe to eat.

Widening his own smile, he swung around slowly so that everyone could get a good look at him. Half a dozen watchers immediately detached themselves from the crowd and left the cafe. They were probably runners being sent off to alert the rest of the town.

He faced the waitress again and asked for a menu. A plastic pin over her heart said JOY.

"Our special tonight is turkey pie with mashed potatoes." She pointed a thumb over her shoulder to show him the grease-penciled note on the mirror behind the counter— *$3.95 with all the trimmings.*

"I'd still like to see the menu, Joy."

"Oh, that's not my name. It's to remind people that they should be happy. Our turkeys are home-grown."

When Traveler didn't respond, somebody in the crowd spoke up. "Wasatch is the *turkey* capital of Sanpete County."

The remark produced a chorus of gobbles.

"Just a hamburger," he said.

"All we've got is turkey pie." The gobbles grew aggressive, wiping away her smile, replacing it with a look of embarrassment.

Rare turkey had been one of his mother's specialities. "That's what I'll have, then."

The waitress sighed with obvious relief and disappeared
through a swinging door into the kitchen. He watched the
crowd in the mirror. They seemed perfectly content to stand
there and watch back. The stare-off continued until the turkey pie arrived. It looked better than it smelled.

He was about to dig in when feet shuffled on the
linoleum floor behind him.

"Here they are," someone said.

Traveler pretended to examine a forkful while watching
the reflected door.

"Nobody messes with the Nibley boys," another man
added.

Christ, he thought, and swung around. The two young
men swaggering through the doorway looked to be just out of
their teens. They wore Levi's rolled up at the cuff, not tai-
lored, and tight knit shirts to show off their biceps. Their
cowboy boots had sharp metal points on the toes. They
could have been the younger brothers of the trio Claire had
sicced on him. Men who bullied their way through life. Angry men afraid of their weaknesses.

Traveler eased off the stool, positioning himself for flight
through the kitchen door. He was a half foot taller than
either Nibley, but they made up for that with a lot of muscle—hard-work muscle, not the showy kind acquired in
gyms. Even so, he figured he could take them. The odds
were against him, though, since everyone in the place would
probably jump him if it came to a fight.

They stopped short when they saw how big he was. But
they weren't going to back off. Not in front of their peers.

"Do you know who we are?" one of them said.

"I heard someone mention the name Nibley."

"That's us." The one talking hooked his thumbs in the
pockets of his Levi's, making himself vulnerable if Traveler
wanted to hit him. The other flexed his finger like a movie
gunfighter. "I'm Mel. This is my kid brother, Junior."

"Ellis Junior," the younger Nibley corrected.

"Neither of us want you poking your nose into our business."

The crowd pressed back against the front window, clearing floor space for action.

"I'm working for your father," Traveler said softly.

"You're leaving town," Mel said.

"You should talk to your father about that."

"We already have."

"And?"

Ellis licked his lips. "Dad isn't himself right now."

"I understand how you feel," Traveler said, stepping forward suddenly with an outstretched hand. "I'm worried about him too."

Caught unaware, Ellis accepted the handshake.

If it weren't for the bystanders, now was the time to hit him and narrow the odds, Traveler thought. They were small-town boys after all; they wouldn't expect that kind of dirty trick.

Traveler wrapped an arm around the young man's shoulder and steered him toward the door. At the threshold he whispered, "Never discuss family business in public."

To save face, Ellis spoke up. "Hey, everybody. This is Nibley business. We want a little privacy."

His brother added, "That's right. We don't want anybody coming out this door in the next few minutes, understand?"

That got a few nods.

By the time the three of them crossed the parking lot to the Nibleys' heavy-duty pickup truck, Traveler was congratulating himself on having defused the situation. That's when Mel's fist caught him on the side of his forehead near the left eye. Traveler staggered but still had sense enough to grab hold of Ellis on the way down. Traveler landed on top. The impact knocked the air out of the boy's lungs.

Traveler shook his head, partly to clear it, and partly to

condemn his own stupidity. These weren't boys. These were men. And Mel had a fist like a roll of quarters. But at the moment, it was the metal tip of Mel's cowboy boot that had Traveler worried.

Traveler rolled. The toe grazed him but caught Ellis in the chest. Bone cracked. Ellis screamed.

Traveler's ears rang. His eyes watered. He blinked, saw Mel moving forward again, and kept on rolling. But he needn't have bothered. Mel had been going to his brother's aid, who was making gasping sounds as he curled into a fetal ball.

"Jesus, Junior, are you all right?"

Junior shuddered. Bone and breath grated.

"Help me, mister. He's dying."

Though still a bit dizzy, Traveler walked on his knees to join them. "Let's sit him up. It will help him breathe."

As soon as they got Ellis righted, his gasps softened to sobs.

"Junior's hurt bad."

"It's a cracked rib, that's all. I've had them. They feel worse than they really are. There's no problem unless you move around a lot and puncture a lung."

"He needs a doctor," Mel said.

"If we can get to a drugstore, we can bandage him ourselves."

"To hell with that. I'm driving him to the doctor's in Ephraim. All I need from you is help to get him into the truck."

"I thought there was a doctor here in Wasatch."

Mel shook his head. "Ephraim's the closest."

"How far?"

"Twenty miles."

"That's a lot of bumps and jolts. I still say we ought to try the drugstore, at least to get him a painkiller."

"There's only one drugstore in town. Old man Odell's place."

Traveler had seen it next to the hotel.

"He's closed this time of night," Mel added.

"If you know where he lives, we can drive by and get him to open up."

"No way. I wouldn't ask him for anything."

"Don't you think you ought to leave that up to your brother?"

Behind them, the cafe's screen door banged. One man came out first, tentatively. Another followed almost immediately. Soon the whole crowd would join them, Traveler knew. He didn't want to be around when that happened. An outsider like himself, a Gentile at that, might get himself lynched.

"What about it, Junior?" Mel said. "Do you want to go to Odell's?"

Ellis grunted "Unh-unh" through clenched teeth.

"All right," Traveler said. "Let's get him into the truck."

Ellis whimpered when they lifted him to his feet.

"Try walking on your own," Traveler said.

"Oh God," he gasped at the first step.

They propped him between them, his arms draped over their shoulders, to ease the burden.

"Try again."

Ellis took a tentative step, panted, and took another. "It's okay," he wheezed. "But Jesus, go slow."

By the time they got him to the truck, the cafe had emptied and the pickup was surrounded. One word from either Nibley and Traveler knew he'd need an ambulance instead of a pickup.

Mel surprised him. "It's all over, everybody. It's my fault that Junior got hurt. Mr. Traveler here is helping me. I'm taking Junior to Ephraim."

"You want company?" someone said.

"There's no need."

When Mel opened the passenger door, light from the Coors neon revealed a turkey-head logo on the side. The bird, with an exaggerated red wattle, was surrounded by a circle of red lettering that spelled out DORITY TURKEY RANCH. The pickup's rear window held a full gun rack, hunters' weapons: a .30-30 lever-action rifle, a pump shotgun, and what looked to be a .30-06.

"You follow me, Mr. Traveler," Mel said and climbed in behind the wheel.

It wasn't until they were out of the parking lot that Traveler started breathing normally again. As a precaution, he followed Mel on the highway out of town. When no headlights appeared in Traveler's rearview mirror, he blinked his high beams, got a honk in return, and then pulled onto the shoulder of the road. He cut his headlights but kept the motor running. After five minutes without traffic in either direction, he U-turned and drove back to the Sleep-Well Motel.

By morning the lump on Traveler's forehead had turned a color he'd never seen before on human skin. Somewhere between green and blue with neon highlights. Gingerly, he tested the bruise with a forefinger. It wasn't as painful as the headache throbbing at the base of his skull. Even his eardrums pulsated with pain. The mosquitoes batting against the window screen sounded like dive bombers from a war movie.

He left the clouded bathroom mirror to sit on the edge of his sagging bed. Once his equilibrium had adjusted to the abrupt change in altitude, Traveler squinted at his watch. It took a moment for the numbers to come into focus. It was nearly nine, the time he'd promised to telephone his father. A safe-arrival call, Martin had called it, but it was more than that. Morning talks were a ritual between them, in person or via Mountain Bell, depending on circumstances.

In broad daylight the motel room looked less cheerful

than the night before. The knotty-pine walls were cracked. So was the Congoleum rug pretending to be Persian. The green shade covering the hanging bulb turned out to be green plastic instead of glass.

Traveler lay back on the prickly bedspread and picked up the phone. Instead of a dial tone, there was a ringing sound. His mind pictured the maze of cords dangling from the switchboard in the office. He was about to go in search of a phone booth when the ringing stopped and Norma Beasley answered. "Did you sleep well at the Sleep-Well Motel?" Her words sounded flat and meaningless.

"I'd like to call Salt Lake," Traveler said. "Could you give me an outside line?"

"I'll have to dial it for you."

Traveler gave her the number, certain that she'd listen in out of boredom if nothing else.

"I was hoping you'd call last night," Martin said as soon as he heard Traveler's voice. "I couldn't sleep worrying about you."

"What could happen to me in a place like Wasatch?"

"The least you could have done was let me know where you're staying."

"I'm calling from the Sleep-Well Motel."

"Sure. You sleep well. I worry."

"What about Claire? Have you come up with anything?"

"You've only been gone a day."

"Come on, Dad. I know you."

"So I did some checking. That doesn't mean I'm Sherlock Holmes."

"Just tell me what you found. Please."

"I dropped by the apartment where you broke that gazooney's leg and talked to the manager. A nice woman. She gave me the eye, I can tell you. I might go back one of these days and ask for a date."

Traveler sighed.

"In her sixties, I'd say, but still with a good figure. Damned good."

"Did you learn anything else?"

"Have you forgotten what I taught you? A good detective doesn't rush in and start asking questions. You do your groundwork first. You set up a relationship, soften them up, then move in for the kill."

Traveler closed his eyes and rubbed the bump on his forehead. He knew better than to interrupt. If he did, it would take even longer to get the information.

"The apartment never belonged to Claire. She showed up with a man on her arm. The pair of them claimed to be engaged and looking for a honeymoon hideaway after the wedding. Those were her words, the manager said. Honeymoon hideaway. Needless to say, they didn't take the apartment. But the man had a card with his name and address. I tried reaching him last night but he wasn't in. If you'd like, I'll try again this morning."

"How did Claire end up using the apartment, then?"

"They stuck gum in the lock, the manager told me. She remembered that Claire was chewing a big wad of bubble gum and getting it all over her chin every time she blew a bubble."

"If the guy with her was in on it, he wouldn't have given out a real card."

"That makes sense."

"Keep checking on him anyway, will you, Dad?"

"I've already got a realtor friend checking his computer for recent rentals. I've also called in a favor with the police department. If Claire's still in Salt Lake, we'll find her sooner or later. You can count on it."

"There's something else," Traveler said.

"I can hear it coming in your tone of voice."

"What?"

"Trouble."

"This time, you're right. I need some information from the State Medical Board."

"You've got to be kidding. I've never had one of those damned doctors talk to me yet. What's this got to do with the Nibley woman's suicide?"

"That's the problem. I don't know. But I met a woman here who mistook me for an investigator from the state board. Apparently she and some others wrote asking for an investigation. It would help if I knew why."

"Probably some malpractice thing or another."

"Maybe."

"Okay. Give me the woman's name."

"Shirley Colton."

"What's the connection with your client?"

"She was a friend of his wife's."

"Do you remember Rule Number Twenty-five?"

Traveler grunted noncommittally. Martin had his rules all right, but the numbers changed with each recitation.

"Coincidence," Martin said. "Never turn your back on one."

"How soon do you think you can get me something from the board?"

"You know doctors. It will probably take me a month to get an appointment. I'd better start now. Call me tomorrow at the usual time."

As soon as Traveler hung up, he went to the office in search of aspirin, catching Mrs. Beasley by surprise nursing her son. The moment she turned away to button her housecoat, Baby Joe started crying. When she faced Traveler again, she was holding the child at arm's length, just beyond the reach of his breast-seeking hands.

"I should have knocked," he said.

"Nat says I shouldn't be embarrassed by something so natural." Her face was as red as her son's hair. "Now what can I do for you, Mr. Traveler?"

He touched his forehead. "If you'd be so kind, I'm in need of some aspirin."

For the first time since he'd entered the office, she looked him in the face. "My God. You look like you need a doctor." The thought seemed to please her.

"A couple of aspirin and some fresh air and I'll be good as new."

She made a face. Her arms were trembling from the strain of holding her son away from her breasts. "My husband and I don't believe in over-the-counter drugs."

She put her son back in his playpen. "A lot of us here in Wasatch stick to home remedies. A Gentile like yourself probably wouldn't believe in such things, but they work. Let me tell you, I've seen miracles."

"What do you suggest for a headache?"

"Prayer."

Traveler had never thought of prayer as a home remedy. "What time does the drug store open?"

"I wouldn't know."

"Isn't there a doctor here in town?" he said, recalling his initial interview with Ellis Nibley. "A Doctor Joe?"

Despite tears, Baby Joe reached through the wooden bars and began tugging at his mother's housecoat.

"Doctor Joe was the answer to our prayers," she said. "He was a saint. I named Baby Joe after him."

At her mention of his name, the boy hit a high, whining note that made Traveler wince.

"Me and my husband were childless for years." Her eyes lost focus. Her faced glowed. Traveler had seen the same look on Willis Tanner's face when he spoke of his work for the prophet, Elton Woolley. "We prayed for help, for guidance. That's where Doctor Joe came in. We went to him for exams and tests. It took a long time, but he never gave up hope. There were times when he got down on his knees and prayed right beside me. God answered our prayers and I had Baby Joe. I named him Josiah Beasley after Doctor Joe."

Her son stopped crying and made a sucking motion with his lips.

She blushed again. "Doctor Joe said long nursing makes a child feel secure."

Baby Joe released his mother's dress to knead the air with his fingers.

Traveler leaned against the lowboy and closed his eyes. Kaleidoscopic flashes of painful light burst against his eyelids.

"Excuse me a moment," she said. "I'll get him a bottle."

Traveler opened his eyes to see the boy shaking his head at that suggestion, but by then his mother was disappearing through the rest room door. Baby Joe turned his attention to Traveler, saw no breasts, and let loose another high-pitched wail. He didn't stop until he was lying on his back in the playpen sucking juice through a rubber nipple.

"When the Lord helped us," Norma Beasley went on as though no time had passed since her previous comment, "I knew me and Nat were close to Godhead."

Her facial glow intensified. Her eyes, showing white, rolled up in search of heaven. "'And the Father and I are one. I am in the Father and the Father in me; and inasmuch as ye have received me, ye are in me and I in you,'" she recited from *The Book of Mormon*.

She tilted her head to one side as if listening to inner voices. Traveler heard voices of his own, childhood voices, Sunday school teachers, his mother, all trying to explain Joe Smith's concept of Godhead. *Man is God in embryo form. As man is, God once was, suffering and struggling toward the knowledge and power that made him God. Thus, man may eventually rule over his own heavenly kingdom, as God rules over us.*

"I'd like to meet Doctor Joe," Traveler said.

The woman clasped both hands over her breasts. "Since the moment you arrived, I've felt a burning in my bosom." She turned and fled through the rest room door once again.

Traveler winked at Baby Joe, but the boy's eyes were

crossed as they tried to fix on the nipple at hand. The only burning in his bosom was likely to be colic.

"You haven't answered my question, Mrs. Beasley," he called.

"I'm listening," she said through the door.

"To me?"

"To God."

To Mormons, a burning in the bosom augurs an insight straight from the Almighty.

"What about Doctor Joe?"

"My husband is cleaning bungalow three. Talk to him."

Nat Beasley had the rumpled, bleary-eyed look of a man caught napping. He stepped across the threshold and closed the door quickly, but not before Traveler saw the unmade bed. Bungalow Three, like his own number six, had knotty-pine walls, a steel-frame bed, and Congoleum on the floor.

Beasley tapped his forehead in the same location as Traveler's bruise. "What happened to you?"

"Is there a doctor in town?"

"You don't look that bad."

"Doctor Joe?" Traveler clarified.

"You'll have to go to Ephraim."

"Is that where I can find Doctor Joe?"

"Follow Highway Eighty-nine and you run right into Ephraim."

"That's not what I asked."

"I have work to do." Beasley backed up until he had the doorknob in hand.

"I'll settle for a supermarket," Traveler said. "Anyplace that sells aspirin."

Beasley slammed the door.

Odell's drugstore had a FOR SALE sign in the window along with a poster advertising a Manti rodeo that had taken place a month ago. The building, two stories of brick trimmed in the town's ubiquitous rock-faced limestone, shared one wall with the Uinta Hotel. The other side faced on a vacant lot and was covered with fading billboards touting long-gone products: *Sonora Phonographs, Studebaker Buggies,* and *Mail Pouch Tobacco.*

As Traveler entered the store, he wondered how long the FOR SALE sign had been up. Months, judging by the flyspecked looks of it.

The siren went off again, not in short bursts like the last time, but in one long continuous blast. The sound was loud enough to make his ears ache. He yawned to relieve the pressure and stepped back outside to look up Main Street. The earlier wisps of smoke in the mountains had been replaced by a tornadolike column rising hundreds of feet in the air. It appeared to be moving downhill toward the town.

Another siren joined in, somewhere from the direction of the sheriff's office.

A block up, several people emerged from the dinette, paper napkins fluttering from their collars. At the same time, Eliza McConkie, the bishop's wife, bustled out of the hotel next door. When Traveler attempted to approach her, she fled up the street.

In need of aspirin more than ever, he started into the drugstore just as a large man wearing a white pharmacist's coat rushed out. His fearful eyes widened at the sight of Traveler.

"My wife's inside," he said. "She'll take care of you."

Traveler grabbed his flabby arm. "I need to talk to you."

"Don't you hear the siren? I'm on call."

"It's about Melba Nibley's prescription."

The man jerked free. "The bishop is waiting for me. We have to set up a first aid station. It's standard procedure."

"Where will you be?"

"Find the bishop and you'll find me." With that, he trotted up Main Street toward the fire station. Two others joined him from the crowd around the Main Street Dinette.

From the doorway a woman said, "You must be the detective."

He turned to see a slim, dark-haired woman, with a weathered sixty-year-old face on a much younger body.

"I'm Cynthia Odell."

He took out his wallet and handed her a card.

"Nobody told me you were named Moroni." She stepped onto the sidewalk and peered toward the mountains. "The weather forecast calls for temperatures in the nineties. I'm afraid we're going to need help from the real Angel Moroni before this fire's out."

"If you're open for business, I'd like to buy some aspirin."

"You see that ridge," she said, pointing to where flames were soaring into the air. "The Dority place is just below there. My husband was alerted an hour ago in case of a wind shift. The poor souls, as if they didn't have enough trouble already."

She read his card one more time before handing it back. "Now what can I do for you, Moroni Traveler?"

"Aspirin."

"You said that already, didn't you. Come inside and I'll fix you up."

The drugstore had a soda fountain along one wall, complete with a gray marble countertop, metal straw dispensers, and a plastic cake cover protecting a doughnut and two sweet rolls from a lazy fly. Traveler climbed onto one of the metal stools and was overwhelmed by the childhood smells of syrups and sodas and phosphates.

"I can fix you a Bromo," she said as soon as she was behind the counter. Her hand caressed a blue plastic dispenser filled with powdered Bromo-Seltzer.

"Just aspirin and a glass of water, if you don't mind."

She thrust a small Coke glass beneath the faucet and pulled the soda jerk's handle.

He watched her image in the mirror behind the counter. "Outside you mentioned something about the Dority place. Is that Louise Dority, Ellis Nibley's daughter?"

"Everybody in town is talking about you and why you're here."

He gave up on Mrs. Odell's reflection to watch her in person. "In my business it's better to catch people by surprise."

Her lined face showed no emotion, but there was a sparkle in her youthful eyes as she slid the glass across the counter. "We've never had a detective in town before, only Sheriff Hickman. Louise must be having a fit, you being here stirring up bad memories. I hear you already met her brothers out at the roadhouse."

"I hope Mrs. Dority is more friendly than they were."

Her lips pursed, fighting a losing battle against a smile. "Those boys have been raising Cain for years. A regular pair of bullies. It's about time somebody cut them down to size. I wish I'd seen that. I hear they had to drive all the way to Ephraim to get themselves attended to."

A fire truck rumbled by, laboring up Main Street toward the mountains.

"We keep the truck parked down behind McConkie's Garage," she said in answer to his questioning look. "There's not enough room at the courthouse."

"Any relation to Bishop McConkie?"

"The same."

"I thought he ran the hotel."

"You mean his wife, Eliza, does. Pearl, one of his others, handles the garage for him."

"Others," he figured, was probably a euphemism for polygamous wives.

"And the fire truck?" he said.

"She keeps that running, too, though how she does it, I don't know. The thing must be forty years old."

"One truck's not going to do much good against a forest fire," he said.

"Half our volunteers are farmers with tractors. Besides, I hear Chief McConkie's already called in help from Ephraim and Manti. Mount Pleasant's on standby."

The siren went off again, causing Traveler to grimace.

"I'm sorry. I forgot your aspirin." She left the counter for the pharmacy area at the back of the store. When she returned she handed him a small tin containing a dozen aspirin.

Traveler took two tablets.

"You ought to have a glass of milk to go with those," she said. "It settles the stomach."

He drained his water glass. "I'm fine. How much do I owe you?"

"Those aspirin have been around a while. They're still marked a quarter."

He examined the tin, looking for an expiration date. If anything, his headache felt worse.

"I'm a practitioner here in Wasatch," she said. "When it comes to the laying on of hands, there's only one better, Jessie Sutton. And she's not seeing anybody these days."

"I'm a Gentile," he reminded her, staring at her large, almost masculine hands.

"From the beginning, Joe Smith commanded us to seek converts to the true church. Maybe you're mine."

He watched in the mirror as she moved behind him, standing so close he could feel her warm breath on the back of his neck. She raised her hands above her head. Her fingers flexed.

"'And whoso shall ask it in my name in faith, they shall cast out devils,'" she murmured, "'they shall heal the sick.'"

Her large fingers fastened on his skull, gripping tightly. He closed his eyes and remembered a healing session his mother had taken him to as a boy. A child, not much younger than Traveler, had been stricken by polio. Doctors had given up. It was only a matter of time. His mother, along with everybody else at the bedside, had condemned the diagnosis with shaking heads. Traveler had shaken his head, too, not wanting to do anything that might hurt the pale child.

The healer was an old man, as white-haired as Santa Claus. Hands pressed together in prayer, he had knelt beside the bed. His hands began to shake as if gathering power. Finally, they fell upon the boy.

"Heal!" the man had commanded. "Heal!"

"Heal!" Cynthia Odell said in Traveler's ear.

He twitched. Her fingers gripped so hard they trembled.

In the mirror he could see her sweating. Her eyes were closed. Her breath was coming faster.

"Heal," she moaned.

A rasping sigh emptied her lungs. Her hands fell away. He let out a sigh of his own.

She dragged herself onto the stool beside him and stared at him in the mirror. "How do you feel?"

He rocked his head experimentally. "Better." His headache had receded to a distant pinpoint.

A smile lit up her face. "At heart you're not a Gentile. You're a believer."

"Did you know Melba Nibley?" he asked.

She peered down at her hands, which lay motionless on the marble countertop. "If you question God's will, the pain will return."

"I'm trying to help Ellis Nibley."

She drew a deep breath. "First Melba, now the fire burning toward the Dority place. I don't know what to think. Maybe that family is cursed."

Traveler concentrated on her image in the mirror. "Do you know any reason why they should be?"

Her eyes found his for an instant before going into hiding. "A lot of people thought Melba was stuck up. But they didn't know her. She was shy, that's all. Especially in high school. Now me, they called Cyn. Spelled with an S, my mother used to say."

"We were all shy in high school," Traveler said.

"Looking at you, Mr. Traveler, I'd say you were one of those who liked gym class. An athlete. But to some it can be hell. I remember our teacher, Miss Brodie. If you ask me, she never fell off the roof in her life."

Traveler was about to ask for an explanation when he remembered his mother using the same expression once or twice, her genteel way of referring to menstruation.

"When any of us tried using that time of month as an

excuse not to dress for gym, she'd say we were imagining things. That or lying to get out of hard work."

Her frankness surprised him.

"I hated her and that damned class," she went on. "Shirley Colton and I used to write excuse notes for each other, signing our mothers' names. But Melba didn't have the nerve. And let me tell you, she went through hell every time she fell off. That and pimples. They plagued her all the way through her junior year. It got so bad she was embarrassed to shower in front of others. Even with me, and I was her closest friend in those days."

The woman caught her breath. "Now that we're talking about it, I remember something else. Another big trauma in our lives. We had to have physical exams every year. It was required to get through high school. They stuck you with needles and took your blood, things like that. And of course, Miss Brodie was always there, shuttling us back and forth to the doctor when he couldn't come on campus. She'd always say, 'Don't be bashful. Your husband's going to see you like this one day.' Easy for her to say. She wasn't married."

Mrs. Odell snorted. "She never did get married either. But then she got her thrills watching us girls in the shower if you ask me. Anyway, those physicals were personal, if you know what I mean. For someone as shy as Melba, they were sheer hell. During senior physicals, she stayed home pretending to be sick. The doctor was a man, of course, and she was scared to death of men. But he caught up with her. I remember that Melba's eyes were red for days from crying."

Her hands came up from the countertop to rub her eyes, as if to erase the sight of those high school memories. Her own eyes were pink when she spoke again. "The plain fact is, I don't remember Melba going on a single date in high school, not until the senior prom with Ellis. If you ask me, he was the only boy she ever went out with."

She spun off the stool and retreated behind the soda fountain, where she busied herself washing Traveler's glass. As she returned it to the shelf below the mirror, he thought that her reflected eyes were more inflamed than rubbing accounted for.

He changed the subject to calm her. "I saw your For Sale sign in the window."

She sighed and turned to face him. "Business is bad."

"Is there another drugstore in town?"

"No."

"Then you have a monopoly."

"You'd think so, wouldn't you? But the general store sells Band-Aids and toothpaste and things like that."

"What about prescription drugs like tranquilizers?"

"I know what you're getting at, Mr. Traveler. You'll have to talk to my husband, Enos, about anything like that. You saw him leaving for the fire department."

"How long have you been trying to sell?" he asked.

"You might as well know it. Enos and I are being shunned."

He hadn't heard that term in years. But then Salt Lake, as the state capital, was less homogeneous and therefore more sophisticated than the rest of rural Utah, where the church accounted for ninety percent of the population.

"It's a religious matter," she added, "something an outsider wouldn't understand."

"You'd be surprised."

She went on without missing a beat. "Of course, if someone gets sick in the middle of the night and needs medicine, that's a different matter. They're on the phone to Enos no matter what the time, begging him to come into the store and fill their prescription." Her lips trembled. "But if it's not an emergency, off they go to the drugstore in Ephraim or Manti."

Traveler wondered if he'd get out of a warm bed to help people who treated him like that. "Why don't you and your husband go on a long vacation and see how folks around here like being without a druggist?"

"Enos wouldn't do that. He's too conscientious. By the way, how's your headache?"

Tentatively, he turned his head from side to side. "I feel fine."

She flexed her fingers. "It's good to know I haven't lost my touch."

"Are they shunning your healing, too?"

"Those that come to me sneak in the back way at night. But if I meet them on the street in broad daylight, they look the other way."

"And you still treat them?"

"It's God's gift to give, not mine." She nodded at the tin of aspirin on the counter. "There's no need for you to buy those."

He handed her a dollar. "It's nice to have painkillers around in case of an emergency."

"You could have got them at Ellis Nibley's General Store."

He smiled. "Not for a quarter."

Her face softened. "Melba used to say the same thing. That we ought to keep up with the times and raise our prices."

"You liked her, didn't you?"

"When I heard she died, part of me died too. At the funeral I couldn't look Ellis in the face. I guess I figured he was to blame one way or another. But the last time I saw him—he came in here despite the shunning to thank me for a casserole I'd sent over the day after she died—my heart melted. He'd aged ten years. On top of that, he hired you, too, didn't he? That counts for something. He must be in the dark as much as the rest of us." Her mouth opened wide as if she were stretching her jaw muscles. "Enos thinks otherwise. He says you being here is Ellis's way of paying conscience money."

She walked away from Traveler to stare out the front window. "Look how dark the town is."

"It's the smoke blotting out the sun."

"That's where you're wrong, Mr. Traveler."

The sky grew darker, the smoke thicker as Traveler drove up Main Street toward the fire. At Taylor Road, he turned south in the direction of the old quarry where much of the county's oolite limestone had been mined. A block shy of the open pits, he swung east on Grant Avenue, and was again heading into the Wasatch Mountains. Cynthia Odell's directions were exact in every detail, even down to the spot where the pavement ran out. At that point, the avenue had changed its name to Dority Canyon Road.

He stopped the car and got out. Smoke had settled over the area like a fog. Visibility was down to fifty yards. For all he knew, flames could be just beyond the edge of sight.

He shook his head at the vista before him. From now on the road narrowed to a single, rutted lane. Waist-high weeds, tinder-dry and waiting for combustion, grew on either side. It was questionable whether or not he'd be able to turn around in case of an emergency.

Taking a deep breath was like smoking half a dozen un-filtered cigarettes at once. The temperature, ninety-six de-grees when he'd left town, felt on the verge of spontaneous combustion.

He climbed back into the Jeep wagon, his father's car actually, switched the air conditioner to high, and drove for-ward. As the interior cooled, the engine temperature rose. It was nearing the red line when he broke free of the under-brush and entered a clearing. The smell of smoke changed to something worse. Burning turkey feathers came to mind.

He braked in front of a wooden gate. The sign on it, *Dority Turkey Ranch* surrounding a red-wattled bird, was the same as he'd seen on the pickup truck that the Nibley broth-ers had been driving.

When Traveler got out to open the gate, he heard the frantic gobbling of turkeys. He couldn't blame them for being nervous.

The thought crossed his mind that he should leave the gate open in case of a quick return. Then again, if it came to a matter of survival, he could always ram his way through the barrier.

A hundred yards beyond the gate he saw the house, a brick box with end-wall chimneys and a porch across the front. The logoed pickup, complete with loaded gun rack, was parked in front. A German shepherd was in the open back.

Traveler pulled in beside the truck and rolled down his window an inch or so. "Good dog."

The shepherd, standing rigidly at attention, stared at him silently. The hair on the back of its neck was standing too. Traveler opened the door but didn't get out.

The shepherd didn't budge either.

"Stay," he said, extending one leg tentatively.

The shepherd's lips curled away from its teeth while its tail wagged. Probably in expectation of a meal, Traveler de-cided and honked the horn to announce his presence.

The Nibley brothers came out onto the porch. In baggy overalls and rubber work boots, they bore little resemblance to last night's attackers. Their expressions were different, too. Fear had replaced aggression. Whether fear of the fire or him he didn't know.

"I'm here to see your sister, Louise Dority," Traveler said without opening the door all the way.

"Come on in," Mel, the one with the broken rib, said. "Woody there wouldn't hurt a fly." Mel was holding himself stiffly, probably because of a bandaged rib cage.

Woody barked at the mention of his name and hopped out of the truck to raise his leg against the Jeep's front tire.

As soon as Traveler got out of the air-conditioned car, his eyes stung and his nose started running. He didn't know which was worse, the smoke or the astringent smell of turkey manure.

"You get used to it," Mel said.

Traveler coughed and shook his head.

"An hour from now you won't even notice it," Ellis Jr. added.

Not trusting their sudden camaraderie, Traveler hesitated at the bottom of the porch steps. "You didn't say if your sister was home or not?"

"Tell him to come in," a woman said from inside the house. "As for you two, go on out and see if you can help Clem with the firebreak."

"Mel ought to stay here," Ellis called back.

Mel hugged his ribs to prove the point.

The woman came to the screen door, which was home to a swarm of large and shiny black flies. She was a big, strong-looking woman, stout not fat, about thirty with gray already streaking her brown hair. She reminded Traveler of a teacher he'd had in grade school.

"You have to be Mr. Traveler," she said.

"Yes, ma'am."

She opened the door carefully so as not to disturb the flies. "You'd better come on in before they do."

As he stepped past her, the smell of vanilla extract canceled out the turkeys and the smoke.

She closed the screen door and latched it.

"One of us ought to stay here with you," Mel said. A whine had crept into his voice.

"I'm not asking you to kill yourself." She planted her hands on sturdy hips. "Just be out there with Clem in case of trouble."

Like scolded children, they hung their heads and trudged away.

She watched until they disappeared in the smoke before closing the inner, glass door. The temperature in the house felt ten degrees cooler than outside.

"Don't think I'm hard-hearted, sending Mel out hurt the way he is. But my husband's all alone up there in the hills."

"Just about every man in town has been called out to help."

"Clem's a volunteer, too. But Dority Canyon is no place for a fire engine. He knows that and so does Chief McConkie. It could get trapped in here."

She pointed east where the mountains would be if they could be seen. "That's why Clem's out there on Axhandle Ridge trying to widen a natural break. Our neighbors have promised to join him when they can. But if the wind keeps blowing, I don't think anybody can stop the fire."

"Could you move the birds?"

"If it came to it, the best we could do is turn them loose, I guess. But turkeys are dumb, so God knows if they could save themselves."

She leaned toward him, her eyes narrowing as she peered into his face. The vanilla scent grew stronger, along with the smell of fresh baking. "What did you do to my brothers last night?"

"I'm sure they've told you."

"They did that, all right. Though I'm not sure I believe them." She shook her head. "Mel's broken bones before, but I've never seen him like this. You took all the fight out of him."

"It's the fire."

"You're a big man, Mr. Traveler. They said you attacked without warning, that they never had a chance."

"You have my word, Mrs. Dority. I didn't start the fight, and I didn't hit him either. Ellis was trying to kick me and got his brother instead."

She looked at him for a moment without saying anything. Then suddenly she smiled. "It's about time. My brothers have been bullies all their lives. When I was growing up, there were times when they made my life miserable. I blame my father. He encouraged them. So does Clem, my husband, I'm afraid. What about you, Mr. Traveler? Are you a bully?"

"A man in my business sometimes has a strange effect on people."

"My brothers are afraid of you. Anyone could see that. That's a first for them. Even so, I'd be careful if I were you. This sudden turnabout on their part may be an act. In any case, you look like a mercenary to me."

"Your father hired me."

"I know that now."

"All I'm trying to do is help him live with what happened."

"What about the rest of us?" She moved to one of the east-facing windows, pulling aside the lace curtain to look out. "Is it my imagination, or can you smell roasting turkeys?"

Traveler took a deep breath. All he could smell was her vanilla scent. It made him hungry.

She swung around, hugging herself. "If the turkeys go, our lives go with them."

"What about insurance?"

"It's never enough, is it?" She wiped her eyes. "You'd think my father would have warned me that you were coming. But no. I had to hear it from the women at the Relief Society. Five or six have called here already. Of course, it would have to be Cynthia Odell who got to me first. If my friends find out I've talked to her . . ."

"Is she a friend?"

"She and her husband are being shunned."

"Why?"

"Do you know what she said? That you weren't as tough as you look. Is that true? Have you got my brothers spooked for nothing?"

"I never argue with a lady."

"Isn't that a man for you." She beckoned him to follow her through a narrow doorway into the kitchen, where the smell of fresh baking was even stronger. They sat facing one another across a scarred wooden table that held a large platter of cookies made in the shape of turkeys. "We call them vanilla gobblers? They're just out of the oven. Help yourself."

The cookie tasted as good as she smelled. Mrs. Dority smiled at his reaction and sat back, her arms folded across her breasts, to watch him eat.

He went through half a dozen gobblers, hoping she'd say something unsolicited, something that might ease the way onto the dangerous ground of suicide.

When that didn't happen, he gave up on the cookies and plunged ahead. "Your father has asked me to find out why your mother took her own life."

"Do you think you can?"

"My initial advice to your father was to forget the whole thing."

"Then why did you come around here pretending to be an investigator from the State Medical Board?"

"That wasn't my mistake."

"It was cruel," she said. "Getting the women's hopes up like that."

"Does this have anything to do with your mother's death?"

The woman opened her mouth as if to speak but her teeth snapped together first.

"Maybe I should talk to your mother's doctor. I understand he's in Ephraim."

"Thank God for that, anyway."

Traveler pretended to concentrate on another cookie while watching her closely. Unless he was mistaken, her face had changed; she looked relieved.

He said, "Shirley Colton told me that she was the one who wrote to the state board. Was it about your mother?"

"That would be for Shirley to say."

Traveler dropped the gobbler back onto its platter. "Let me be blunt, Mrs. Dority. Do you have any idea why your mother might have killed herself?"

"No," she said flatly.

Too flatly, he thought.

"For your father's sake, why don't you tell me what's going on?"

"If I had anything to say, I'd say it to Dad's face, not to you, a Gentile."

"Sooner or later, I'll find out what it is that you're hiding," he said, although he knew damn well the odds were against an outsider like himself.

"I was born into the church, Mr. Traveler. I've been a member in good standing ever since I was old enough to make that decision for myself. I abide by our covenants. When the Bishop's Court said it was over, that was good enough for me."

Outside, the smoke glowed, giving Traveler the impression that hellfire was about to break through. For a moment he thought about going back for Mrs. Dority, but she'd already disappeared in the direction of the firebreak, carrying cookies and cold milk to her family.

The Dority turkeys, judging from their frenzied gobbling, needed rescuing too. But all he could do was start up the Jeep, switch on its headlights, and go back the way he came.

He met the fire truck at the intersection of Taylor Road, where Dority Canyon Road changed back into Grant Avenue. The truck, dating from the forties by the look of it, was parked facing downhill away from the mountains.

Harold McConkie, fire chief and bishop, was standing on its hood peering through binoculars toward the Wasatch Plateau. The druggist, Enos Odell, was perched on the running board in his white smock. Two other men wearing helmets and knee-length flame-retardant coats and yellow hard hats waited nearby.

Traveler pulled well off the road and stopped. By the time he got out, McConkie was back on the ground and waving at the pair with helmets to spread out. One went south, the other north along Taylor Road. Both stopped about fifty yards beyond the intersection, looked back at McConkie, and waved.

Only then did the bishop acknowledge Traveler's presence. "I've declared this to be a fire zone. Civilians must clear the area."

"If you need an extra hand, say so."

McConkie shook his head. It wasn't a negative gesture, but one of resignation. "I've got men posted all along here. Close enough so they can hand-signal one another when they see flames. Right now we don't know where we're going to make our stand." He held up a portable two-way radio. "I wouldn't need to spread my men out if we had enough of these to go around. Now what is it you want from me?"

Traveler glanced at Odell, then shrugged.

"Don't play coy. You could have driven on by but you didn't." McConkie adjusted his hard hat. CHIEF was stenciled on the front in bold black letters. Wrinkles puckered his normally placid face.

"The Dority family needs help," Traveler said. "They're trying to cut their own firebreak back up the canyon."

"Clem knows I can't risk our only engine on that road. Not when we might need it in town."

He gestured toward the houses and barns scattered along Taylor Road. "A block from here homes are cheek to cheek. It hasn't rained in a month. Their roofs are dry as tinder. I've got every man in town on standby. As soon as I know where we're going to fight, we'll stake out our command post and Enos here will organize a first aid station."

"I hate to ask at a time like this," Traveler said, "but I need a couple of minutes with Mr. Odell."

McConkie nodded as if he'd suspected Traveler's intention all along. "Two minutes, no more." He walked far enough away to be out of earshot.

Traveler turned his back to McConkie before speaking to the druggist. "Your wife tells me you're being shunned."

"That's my business. What's yours?"

"It's Melba Nibley. I'm sure you know that already. Now why don't you begin by telling me how she got enough tranquilizers to kill herself?"

"I fill prescriptions. I don't make decisions."

"And her prescription?"

"That's confidential information. You'd have to speak with her doctor."

Before Traveler could reply, the bishop shouted, "Hallelujah! The wind's shifted."

It was blowing uphill, away from the center of Wasatch. It carried Odell's astringent drugstore smell, much like that of the dentist from Traveler's childhood.

McConkie came running, breathing noisily through his mouth. When he reached Traveler and Odell, he took off his hard hat. Sweat had plastered his gray hair against his scalp. "Thank God. That usually happens this time of afternoon, but I've been praying just the same." His facial wrinkles dissolved away, leaving the worry-free bishop behind.

"Are you the only bishop in town?" Traveler asked.

"That's right, son. Wasatch isn't big enough for more than one ward."

"Then it would be up to you to convene a bishop's court?"

"That's church business."

"My question was theoretical."

"I suspect you know the answer already."

What Traveler knew was that a bishop's court, the kind mentioned by Louise Dority, was called only as a last resort. Those found guilty could be put on probation or, in the case of more serious religious transgressions, denied temple access.

Without such access there could be no celestial marriage, no binding together for eternity, and no baptisms to raise dead ancestors from hell. A bishop's court could even lead to excommunication, though not without higher approval from the Council of Seventy or the Apostles, perhaps even Elton Woolley himself depending on the religious crime involved.

"I understand a bishop's court was convened here in Wasatch quite recently."

McConkie glanced at the druggist. "Who told you that?"

"It's something I heard."

"Telling you was a breach of faith. I'll have whoever did it up before another court."

"You admit it, then."

"Come with me."

McConkie led the way back to the fire engine, where he invited Traveler to climb up on top with him. From there, they had a view, though somewhat murky, of most of Wasatch.

"When our forefathers built this town," the bishop said, "they followed Joseph Smith's guidelines explicitly." He blinked at Traveler with eyes as murky as the atmosphere. "The cities of Zion, our first prophet called them, were set out precisely so that everything revolved around the church."

He pointed due west. "I quote the prophet. 'Fill up the world in these last days, and let every man live in the city, for this is the city of Zion.' When Brigham Young visited Wasatch in 1872, he took my grandfather by the hand—I have an old photograph to prove it—and congratulated him on a job well done."

"That's something to be proud of," Traveler said, "but it doesn't answer my question." He brushed the hair out of his eyes, but the wind blew it right back.

"My ancestors were original settlers here, Mr. Traveler.

I'm a third-generation bishop. That makes me and my family responsible for what's happened."

"And what's that?" Traveler asked, pretending to study the town while watching McConkie out of the corner of his eye.

"Some call it progress. I call it deviation from Joseph Smith's master plan."

"About the court?" Traveler persisted.

"I cannot break faith. If you want information, you'll have to petition the church offices in Salt Lake."

"That's impossible. I'm a Gentile."

"I knew that the moment I laid eyes on you."

McConkie was staring at Traveler's hair, which was long by Utah's rural standards.

"You look like a Catholic to me, Mr. Traveler."

Traveler smiled. "I always thought one Gentile was much like another."

"I remember something my father once told me. 'Harold,' he said, 'do you know why you never see a bald-headed Catholic?' 'No, Dad,' I said. 'Tell me.' 'Because, son, they're the spawn of the devil and need hair to hide their horns.'"

When Traveler got back to the Sleep-Well Motel, Nat Beasley was on duty. His soot-streaked face and dusty clothes said he'd just come off the fire line. The office smelled of smoke and used diapers. There was no sign of either his wife or Baby Joe.

"Your father called," Beasley said. "He said he'd call back about six. Six is when we close down the switchboard for dinner."

"Can't you keep the line to my room open?"

Beasley pointed to a small folded sign on the countertop. "'Switchboard hours,'" he read, "'are nine to noon and two to six, except by special arrangement.'"

"All right. I'm asking for special arrangements."

"We had someone hurt on the fire line. I had to drive him over to Ephraim to be treated. Otherwise, I wouldn't have been here to answer the phone at all and you wouldn't have gotten the message."

"Every town needs its own doctor."

Beasley snorted. "If you want to call your father, you'd better do it now, before I go back to the fire."

"What about your wife?"

"She won't be answering the switchboard for a while either. She and Baby Joe volunteered to help make turkey sandwiches and lemonade at the Relief Society."

"Is it all right if I call from my room?" Traveler asked.

Beasley shrugged. "If you want privacy, there's a pay phone down the road at the Wasatch Cafe."

Traveler took out his wallet, extracted a twenty-dollar bill, and laid it on the lowboy. "I'm willing to pay for your special arrangements."

"If I plug in an open line to your room, there's no telling how many long-distance calls you might make."

Traveler laid down another twenty.

"We'll still have to bill you for any toll calls."

"Agreed."

Beasley fiddled with the switchboard for a moment. "You're all set."

Traveler went to his cabin and sat on the front step where he could keep an eye on the office. He'd killed half a dozen mosquitoes and donated blood to half a dozen others by the time Beasley drove away in his car.

Brushing himself free of bugs, Traveler fled inside to check the phone for a dial tone. After that, he showered, changed clothes, and then lay on the bed waiting for Martin's call. A rumbling stomach reminded him that he hadn't eaten anything since Louise Dority's cookies.

The phone rang at six exactly.

"I've got good news and bad news," Martin said. He sounded like he was eating something.

"Hold on a moment," Traveler said. He got up, went to the bathroom, and drank two glasses of water to keep his stomach quiet. As soon as he picked up the phone again, he asked for the bad news first.

"I contacted the State Medical Board like you asked. I told them the usual story, that lives were at stake. They told me to put any request for information in writing and they'd get back to me."

"You sound like you're eating peanuts," Traveler said.

"Cashews actually."

"What's the good news?"

"I found an old friend of Claire's, a man named Homer Young."

"I never knew her to have old friends, only new ones."

"He's the one who left his card at the apartment where you were attacked. He claims he hasn't heard from her since then. I believe him. Oh, there's one more thing. When I asked him if he knew where she was now, he said, 'The last thing she told me was that she was going home soon.'"

"Where's home?"

"Young asked Claire the same thing. 'I'm going home to Moroni,' she said. At first he figured that meant you. But later on he got to thinking about it and decided she meant the town of Moroni. He says she once told him that her family used to live there, but that all the Bennions had finally moved away."

"That doesn't get us much closer to the boy."

"The best thing I could think of was to follow her. That's why I came to Moroni. I'm there now, twenty miles away from you."

"And?"

More chewing sounds came down the line. "I've located a relative of sorts, but I thought you'd want to be here when I knocked on the door."

"What about Claire?"

"If she's here, I figure her to be staying with the relative."

Traveler was torn. He didn't feel up to coping with Claire
or her relatives at the moment. At the same time, it would
take two of them if they were to have any chance at all of
getting information out of Claire should she be there.

"I'll be with you in thirty minutes."

Topping a rise in the road, Traveler saw the town of Moroni nestled against the north bend of the San Pitch River. A couple of miles later Highway 116 changed into Main Street. Following Martin's directions, Traveler passed the Moroni Tithing Office on the southwest corner of the town square and turned onto Jabez Avenue. His father's Ford was parked in front of the third house on the right. All Claire had to do was look out a parlor window and be forewarned.

The house dated from the 1870s, one of those practical brick structures with chimneys at both ends. When he knocked, Martin opened the heavily paneled front door. A short stout woman, no more than five feet tall, stood beside him. She was probably Martin's age, though her face was wrinkled enough for a hundred-year-old.

"This is Miz Neff," he said, pronouncing "Mrs." the rural Utah way. "She saw me parked out front, took pity and invited me in."

"Everybody around here calls me Ma Neff," she said. "I'm not really anybody's ma, but Claire started calling me that when she came to live with me. A few people call me the widow Neff," she added with a wink in Martin's direction. "You can call me Dora."

Martin rolled his eyes in mock protest. "We missed Claire. She was staying here until last night but then took off."

"Come on in," the woman said. "Dinner's on the table. I've got a roast I bought for Claire. Since she's not here I need help eating it. Besides, I like feeding hungry men."

The oak dining room set was nearing the prerequisite years to become a collectible antique. So was the Woolworth china.

"Carving's a man's job," she told Martin when she set the roast beef in front of him.

A knife and sharpening rod had already been set out next to his place setting. While he carved, she dished out mashed potatoes and gravy, carrots and string beans.

"This was Claire's favorite dinner when she was with me," the woman said.

"When was that?" Traveler asked.

"Through her last three years of high school. You see, her family used to live next door, where the vacant lot is now. But when they moved to Salt Lake, Claire didn't want to go with them. She can be very stubborn, you know."

Traveler nodded. Claire had seldom spoken to him of her childhood. Usually, she did it in the calm after sex.

"She didn't want to get lost in a big high school in Salt Lake," Ma Neff went on. "After all, she had her friends here in Moroni."

"I was abandoned as a little girl," Claire had told him once. *"I used to stand at the window all day waiting for them to come back and find me. But they never did."*

"Where is Claire now?" Traveler asked.

"Lord knows. I wish I did. She went off to meet someone last night, or so she said, and hasn't been back since."

"Who was she going to meet?"

The woman heaped a second helping of potatoes on Martin's plate before answering. "I don't know. I got the impression she was driving over to Wasatch."

"Why?"

"I don't remember exactly. She must have said something during the day, but my memory isn't what it used to be."

"One thing's for sure," Martin said. "You remembered how to cook the best roast beef I've ever tasted."

While Ma Neff beamed, Traveler thought over the situation. Knowing Claire, Wasatch was the perfect destination. There, she could put the screws to him one more time and get even for her loss in court.

Traveler led the way to Wasatch driving the Ford, his father following in the Jeep. Flames from the forest fire had been visible from as far away as the Moroni junction where 116 ran into U.S. 89.

By the time they pulled into the Sleep-Well Motel, it was nearly midnight. The NO VACANCY neon out front paled in comparison to the red glow coming off the fiery mountains.

The crunch of an extra set of tires on the gravel track leading to the cabins brought Mrs. Beasley outside, carrying a sleeping Baby Joe in her arms. Pink curlers stood out in her hair like night crawlers. A man's plaid overcoat was draped around her shoulders. Her white nylon nightgown hung all the way to her bare feet.

"Don't think because my husband's still out on the fire that you can put anything over," she said, picking her way gingerly across the gravel. "You paid for a one-man room. Guests cost extra."

"This is my father," Traveler said.

"Man and wife can share a room at the same price. All others pay extra."

"I have to put up with a grown son living at home," Martin said. "I want my own room when I go on vacation."

"How's the fire doing?" Traveler asked.

Baby Joe opened his eyes. Immediately, Mrs. Beasley repositioned him in the crook of her arm so she'd have one hand free to wave mosquitoes away from his face.

"They're evacuating some of the outlying homes and ranches now," she said. "That's why I've got the No Vacancy sign on. We expect refugees if the ward house and the hotel can't hold them."

"What about me?" Martin said.

"Like I said, you'll have to pay extra. In advance." She started back toward the office, tiptoeing like someone walking over hot coals. "You'll have to sign in, too."

They let Mrs. Beasley get out of earshot before following her toward the office.

"Unless we find Claire," Traveler said, hanging back, "a couple more days in Wasatch ought to do it."

"Does that mean you've come up with something to help that man, Nibley?"

"Hell, no. I'm being stonewalled wherever I go. When people do talk to me, I can't figure out what's going on. Small towns are bad enough anywhere, but in Utah they're impossible. A bishop's court has been held and letters have been written to the State Medical Board. How the hell am I'm going to get information out of doctors or the church?"

Ahead of them, the office lights came on.

"So what are you going to do now?" Martin said, flailing at mosquitoes.

"Go home if I don't get a break pretty soon. Tomorrow

I'll check out Melba Nibley's medical records. Since there's no doctor here in town, that means a trip to Ephraim."

Martin grunted. "Claire or no Claire, if I'd known about these damn bugs I'd have stayed in Moroni. Your old dad hasn't lost his touch. The widow Neff offered to put me up for the night."

"Claire said the same thing the first time I met her."

When Traveler entered the Sleep-Well's office the next morning, Mrs. Beasley was bent over a quilt that covered the entire lowboy. The quilt's intricate design looked to be a map of Wasatch, with stylized roads, buildings, and a very prominent church. The colors of the landmarks varied. But the only time red appeared was in the figures, all skirted to denote the female sex. Centered at the bottom of the quilt was a hand-stitched legend that said ZION.

"That must have taken a long time," he said.

"I've been working at it since I came of age," she answered without looking up. "And now finally I can finish it."

"What's it to be, a bedspread?"

She shook her head. "A history."

"I see," Traveler said noncommittally, figuring that any further interest on his part might lead to theology. "I need directions. I'm driving over to Ephraim today to see a Dr. Gourley. When I talked to Ellis Nibley on the phone last night, he told me the doctor had his wife's medical records."

"Joe Gourley has been taking care of Baby Joe for some time now." She raised her head from the quilt to make kissing noises at the child, who was sitting in his playpen watching Traveler.

"What's his address?"

"I don't really know, though I've been there a dozen times. It's right on Main Street in the center of town, next to the bank. If you need help, ask anybody. They'll know where he is."

Outside, Martin was sitting behind the wheel in the Jeep. "I decided to take my own car for once," he said.

"I may need the four-wheel drive if I have to go into the hills again."

Martin sighed, got out, and headed for the old Ford. "I wish you'd get your damned air conditioning fixed."

"You said you didn't believe in it, that air conditioners pollute the atmosphere."

"There you go again, quoting me."

"There's a garage here in town, McConkie's. You're welcome to take the Ford in."

"I'm on my way back to Moroni to check on Claire."

"Checking on the widow Neff is more like it."

"I'll call the motel with any messages."

"Nothing complicated," Traveler advised. "With any luck I ought to be back from Ephraim in a couple of hours."

Ephraim was very much like Wasatch, or Moroni for that matter. Its offices and stores, its public buildings, built of the ubiquitous oolitic limestone, clustered in a four-block area around the intersection of Main and Center Streets. Traveler parked in front of the Towne Theater, which had somehow escaped the oolite. Its marquee advertised shows Thursday through Saturday.

"Sunday movies are a sin," Traveler's mother had said every Saturday night to forestall argument. "As bad as drinking Coke-Cola or smoking."

He crossed Main to the United Order Co-op, built in 1864 as an offshoot of Salt Lake's Zion's Cooperative Mercantile Institution, ZCMI to the faithful. The derelict Co-op bore an inscription above the door, HOLINESS TO THE LORD. A contractor's sign out front, faded over the years, said RESTORATION IN PROGRESS.

Farther down the block he found the doctor's office. It was on the first floor of a two-story adobe hiding behind a Victorian false front.

Traveler shook his head the moment he walked into the waiting room. But nothing changed. The time-warped illusion continued. Turn-of-the-century love seats, upholstered in rose velvet, faced each other across an Edwardian table strewn with *Reader's Digests*.

One love seat was empty. The other contained a mother and child. Traveler bypassed them for the nurse's window, where he was told he'd have to wait his turn.

Forty-five minutes later he was ushered into an office as modern as the computer on the desk. Dr. Gourley was somewhere between time periods, about fifty and starting to go gray. Half-glasses were perched at the top of his forehead.

Traveler identified himself. "I represent Ellis Nibley, who's asked me to look into the death of his wife. He said you had her records."

"She wasn't a patient of mine. I hope you understand that."

"You're Dr. Joseph Gourley, aren't you? Doctor Joe?"

The man clucked sympathetically. "It's an easy mistake to make. Josiah Sutton was Doctor Joe. Everyone called him that, myself included. He died a week ago yesterday."

"How?"

Gourley lowered his half-glasses into place. The thick lenses obscured his eyes. "I don't see that that has anything to do with Mrs. Nibley."

"Curiosity is a habit with me."

"You've got to understand something about this part of

the state. About Sanpete County. Things don't change around here. At least not very fast. I was born and raised right here in Ephraim, but I went away to college. I stayed away to practice medicine, too. Until a year ago when my father died. That's when I came back to take over his practice. I thought it was my obligation. My father always said it was. But you know what happened? Half my father's patients walked out on me without giving me a chance. They switched over to Doctor Joe. The other half still consider me an outsider. About the time I'm ready to retire they may accept me back into the fold. If I'm lucky."

He lowered his head to peer over the glasses, which began a slow slide down his nose as he spoke. "You see, Doctor Joe and my father were institutions in these parts. Their practices took in just about all of Sanpete County. Doctor Joe was centered in Wasatch but still covered Moroni, Freedom, Wales, and even Jerusalem. That's a lot of territory, especially when you consider the fact that he made house calls like my father. Hell, so do I. A doctor couldn't live on a one-town practice in this county."

When the glasses reached the end of Gourley's nose, he halted their progress with a forefinger without pushing them back into place. "All the house calls in the world won't make you a rich man in this part of Utah. Sanpete's a depressed area. Has been for years. At the rate the population's shrinking, there won't be anybody left before long. It's no wonder we can't get new doctors to settle here."

"Are you sorry you came back home?" Traveler said.

"Unfortunately I don't have a son to follow in my footsteps."

That surprised Traveler, since Mormons made Catholics look barren when it came to family size. "Doctor Joe's death must be going to help your business."

Gourley smiled and raised his glasses back onto their hairline perch. "You make that sound like a motive for getting rid of the competition."

Traveler smiled back. "I don't know how he died yet."

"What do you know about Doctor Joe?"

"Not much. Only that there seem to be two points of view about him. You say he was an institution. Others I've talked to have called him a saint. Someone else said he was the devil incarnate, or words to that effect."

Gourley snorted. "Doctors are like anyone else. When they save lives, they're called saints. When they lose one, through no fault of their own usually, they make enemies."

He straightened his shoulders to take a deep breath. Exhaling made him sag. "In Doctor Joe's case I guess it doesn't matter anymore. So you might as well hear it from me as anyone else. The man hanged himself."

"A week ago?"

"That's what I said. A week ago yesterday."

"It's strange that nobody's mentioned it to me before."

"People don't like bringing up painful subjects. Besides, the man was sick. Cancer. I didn't make the diagnosis myself, but his wife told me the details when I called her. It hit me hard, I'll tell you. I don't remember a suicide in these parts before."

"But Melba Nibley killed herself."

He shook his head. "You must be mistaken. The bishop himself told me her death was from natural causes."

"Did you believe him?"

"I signed the death certificate, didn't I?"

"That doesn't answer my question," Traveler said.

"That's all you're going to get from me on the subject of Melba Nibley. Like I told you before, she wasn't really my patient. Her records were forwarded to me for the autopsy."

Traveler checked back at the motel shortly before noon. Mrs. Beasley was stitching a second black-thread cemetery marker in the upper right-hand corner of her quilt. Baby Joe, his red curls a bright contrast to his mother's dull black hair, was chewing on an empty wooden spool.

"Your father came back half an hour ago," she said.

"I don't see his car."

"He left again. I sent him over to the Co-op." She knotted her thread and snipped off the ends with a pair of embroidery scissors. "I was tempted to put a skull and crossbones for the cemetery but settled for simple crosses in the end. More tasteful, don't you think?"

Traveler nodded. "Why the Co-op?"

"That's where the ladies from the Relief Society are fixing lunch for the men on the fire lines. I thought your father might want to help shuttle the food."

"Your husband said you were helping with the sandwiches."

"I do what the bishop tells me."

"He sent you here?"

She didn't have to answer the question. Her eyes did it
for her. She was following orders. Probably the town fathers
wanted Martin where they could keep an eye on him. Traveler, too, for that matter.

Mrs. Beasley bent over her quilt rather than look Traveler in the face. "I'd be at the Co-op yet if it weren't for the
fact that Baby Joe is coming down with a cold."

She gave up on her handiwork to point at the telephone
switchboard. Cables had been plugged into every slot. "We
have firemen from Manti and Mount Pleasant sleeping in our
cabins right now. That's why the bishop asked us to keep the
phones plugged in twenty-four hours a day, in case someone
has to get through in a hurry."

"Your quilt looks as accurate as a road map," he said.

"Wasatch is laid out according to the words of the
prophet Joseph Smith. Each plat of land is a square mile.
Each block is forty rods square. The streets are eight perches
wide. I walked every street myself, but all I really had to do
was follow the prophet's plan."

"You're the one to ask, then. Where would I find Dr. Joe
Sutton's house?"

Mrs. Beasley shook her head. "That poor woman's had
enough trouble. I won't go adding to it by sending you over."

"I can look it up in the phone book."

"Maybe so, but it won't be on my conscience."

The Wasatch Co-op, on Main just down from the library,
was two stories of grim oolite limestone, overlaid with Victorian trim made of dogtooth brick. Each story had two windows, with sharp dogtooth sills to discourage burglars. The
single, deep-set door reminded Traveler of a tunnel entrance.
When he approached it, Sheriff Mahonri Hickman emerged
from its shadowed interior.

"It's just as I predicted," he said. "You're making people

angry wherever you go. You and your father. He's inside, by the way, making out like a judge sampling wares at the state fair."

"Who's mad at me?"

"The Nibley boys for one."

"I never threw a punch."

Hickman tugged hard enough on the tips of his mustache to create a smile. "If you ask me, I think they got to brooding about you making fools out of them. Not thirty minutes ago, I caught them cruising around town looking for you. They'd been drinking, so I had to take their guns away. Around here, that's serious. Drinking, not the guns."

"Where are they now?"

"They weren't so drunk I couldn't order them back on the fire line. They wouldn't have gone except that I threatened them with a bishop's court."

"I didn't realize ecclesiastical matters were within your jurisdiction."

"There's a lot you don't know about this town and how it runs."

"I know one thing. You could have saved me a lot of trouble if you'd told me about Doctor Joe killing himself."

"That has nothing to do with Melba Nibley. Besides, you didn't ask."

"I've been told nobody ever killed themselves in Wasatch before."

"You find someone dead and who's to say it wasn't natural causes or an accident? As long as there's nothing illegal, that's God's problem, not mine. Take Doctor Joe, for instance. I don't count him as a suicide. He had cancer. Who can blame him for hurrying things along? For all we know, Melba was sick and did the same thing?"

"What about autopsies?"

"Doc Gourley over in Ephraim took care of all that."

"Natural causes in both instances, I assume?"

"Like I said, son, around here we leave judgments to God."

Inside, the Co-op was alive with women, thirty or forty of them at least, swarming around a line of picnic tables laden with food. They spoke in murmurs like women in church, creating a kind of hum that rose and fell almost rhythmically. When half a dozen of them manhandled another table into place, the others formed a kind of bucket brigade to hand along casserole dishes until that table, too, was filled.

The Co-op itself was one large room with whitewashed oolite walls and a worn wooden floor. It reminded Traveler of the basement meeting hall where he'd first attended Sunday school.

Several women glanced his way but kept on working once they saw he wasn't a fireman, wasn't one of their own. He moved along the back wall, out of the bustle, and joined his father, who was sitting alone with a paper plate of food balanced on his lap.

"You've got to hand it to them," Martin said. "The Relief Society is better than the National Guard when it comes to mobilizing for an emergency."

He offered his plate to Traveler, who took half a turkey sandwich.

"Listen to them, Mo. Humming like bees. No wonder the beehive's our state symbol." He gestured toward the line of tables. "Here comes your lunch, if I'm not mistaken."

Traveler looked up to see Shirley Colton and another woman threading their way through the crowd, heading his way. Mrs. Colton was carrying a paper plate, the other a Styrofoam cup.

Martin spoke into his son's ear. "Before she gets here, you ought to know that Claire called Dora Neff while I was in Moroni. She said she was staying over here in Wasatch for the time being. That's why I came back."

The women arrived before Traveler had time to respond. They handed him the plate and cup.

"I'd feel better if I paid," he said.

"I tried that too," Martin said. "They wouldn't let me."

"This is Alice McConkie," Shirley Colton said. "I've asked her to talk to you for me."

The woman was plump, gray haired, red cheeked, and enough like Eliza McConkie, who ran the Unita Hotel, to be a sister. Only sisters didn't share married names.

"I can see it on your face, Mr. Traveler," Mrs. McConkie said. "I'm the bishop's second wife. And no, he's not divorced. My husband believes in the sanctity of revelation. Joseph Smith's word on marriage cannot be revoked merely to satisfy man's laws."

Or his polygamous lust, Traveler thought. That, too, must have shown on his face, because she glared at him and tried to back away. But Shirley Colton held her in place.

"All right, Shirley. You don't have to push. I'll talk to him like I promised. Come with us, Mr. Traveler. We don't have a lot of time to waste and it's best to speak somewhere else."

Traveler glanced at his father.

"Don't worry about me," Martin said.

Traveler followed the pair to the far corner where a quilt frame had been set up. The woman sitting in front of it, with her back to the room and the emergency preparations going on within it, went on with her needlework, ignoring their arrival. Light from an open window behind the frame illuminated the quilt, a replica of the one Norma Beasley was working on at the motel. A smoky breeze rippled the fabric.

"This is Jessie," Mrs. McConkie said. The woman nodded but kept her back to them. "We can speak in front of her."

Jessie, her head bent close to the quilt, was stitching a red devil in the sky above a black-outlined church. The devil was fighting with an angel sewn in gold thread. The angel carried a hangman's noose.

"I didn't expect to see the devil included in a map of Wasatch," Traveler said.

"The devil is a Gentile," Mrs. McConkie replied. "Like yourself. I thank God the bishop isn't here right now. He'd feel obliged to fight you, despite your size, for lying to Shirley here. For telling her that you were from the medical board."

Traveler gazed at Mrs. Colton, who blushed and turned away to keep from looking at him. "I'm sure Mrs. Colton will tell you that I said no such thing. She made that assumption on her own."

"You could have told her the truth," Mrs. McConkie said.

"You're right, of course, and I apologize. My only excuse is that I did it because I thought I might learn something about Melba Nibley by keeping quiet."

"And did you?"

"That's the problem. Nobody's being honest with me either."

"We owe you nothing," the bishop's wife said. "Nothing at all."

"What about Ellis Nibley? Or his wife, for that matter?"

"I represent the Relief Society in this, Mr. Traveler." She half turned and nodded toward the women who were adding the finishing touches to their meal preparation. "All of us think it best that you leave town immediately."

"The sooner you tell me what's going on around here, the sooner I can do just that."

The women exchanged glances. Jessie's needle stopped in midair, hovering over the devil.

"What specifically do you have in mind?" the bishop's wife said.

"To start with, why do you think Melba Nibley killed herself?"

The woman shook her head, whether out of ignorance or refusal he didn't know.

"All right, then," he said, "tell me about Dr. Joe Sutton."

She shook her head again, this time in unison with Shirley Colton. Out of the corner of his eye he saw Jessie's needle plunge into the devil.

"Well, maybe you can tell me about the letters to the medical board then."

"You're an outsider," Mrs. McConkie said, her voice rising to compete with the hum inside the Co-op. "You don't understand what our husbands expect of us. What the church expects."

Traveler glanced around. The humming had stopped. As one, the ladies of the Relief Society were staring at him.

"If we make a formal complaint against you with Sheriff Hickman, he knows better than to oppose the Society."

Mrs. McConkie had been looking past him as she spoke.

When Traveler turned to follow her gaze, a woman in a ging-ham apron left the crowd and came toward him.

"I'm Hope Leary," she said when she got within range.

"Our town librarian," Mrs. McConkie clarified.

"I'm the only other Gentile in town beside yourself," Hope Leary added. "The only single woman too, for that matter, and Catholic to boot. The ladies think that makes me uniquely qualified to give you some advice."

She was in her fifties, he guessed, and reminded him of his third-grade teacher. Except for the gleam in her eye. That was something she had in common with Claire.

"I'm listening," he said.

"Whatever fees you're expecting will be paid. You have the Relief Society's word on it. Since you're a professional, that should be the end of it. Your reason for staying is re-moved."

"A professional can only be fired by his client."

"Do you think Ellis Nibley will stand up against the Re-lief Society?"

Traveler looked around the room and saw grim deter-mination on every face.

"I think you know the answer already," the librarian said. "My advice is to leave Wasatch as quickly as possible."

"When people try to get rid of me, I know they're hiding something."

"Our secrets are our own, Mr. Traveler."

Now was not the time to argue, he knew. And certainly not the place. But he wasn't about to let himself be run out of town. He was about to say so when Martin dragged him from the Co-op.

Traveler and his father hurried up Main Street. When certain they weren't being followed, they settled on the city hall's ash-covered limestone steps. They were facing east toward the burning mountains.

Traveler replayed the women's conversation for his father, including the news of Doctor Joe's death.

"Two suicides in a town this size," Martin said, shaking his head. "I don't like the sound of it."

"Doctor Joe did know he was dying, so he had plenty of incentive. As for Melba Nibley, I don't know any more about her motives than I did to start with. Then again, I'm hardly a father-confessor to the people around here."

"At least we've got one person on our side. Dora Neff is phoning around for me right now, talking to people who wouldn't open up to Gentiles like you and me. If Claire's anywhere in the neighborhood, Dora will find out."

"It had better be soon," Traveler said, "because I have a

feeling Ellis Nibley will be terminating my services any time now."

"Dora would put us up. We could always stay over with her and do research on Claire from there. Come to think of it, what kind of stepmother do you think Dora Neff would make for a son your age?"

Traveler stared at his father. "That's not funny. Not considering our luck with women."

"Maybe that's your problem. This town is nothing but women."

Before Traveler could reply, a phalanx of volunteer firemen turned the corner and came striding toward them. There were about a dozen of them, as black faced and soot-covered as coal miners. Most likely they were coming off the fire line to eat at the Co-op. But instead of looking exhausted, they marched with heads high, shoulders back, singing a Mormon song Traveler remembered from Sunday school, a hymn the pioneers sang while pulling their hand-carts the thousand miles from Missouri to Salt Lake.

"Obedient to the Gospel call
We serve our God, the All in All,
    We hie away to Zion.
We do not wait to ride all day
But pull our handcarts all the way
    And Israel's God rely on.
To Zion pull the handcart
    While singing every day
The glorious songs of Zion
    That haste the time away."

Martin hummed along until the volunteers were out of sight and earshot.

When he grew quiet, Traveler asked, "Do you remember when I quit Sunday school?"

Martin nodded. "I thought your mother'd have a conniption fit. How old were you anyway?"

"Six."

Martin raised his hand as if he were making a toast. "Are you listening, Kary?"

"I told you I couldn't believe what they were teaching me. Do you remember what you told me then?"

"That maybe it was because you were too smart."

Traveler nodded. "Maybe it's the reverse."

"That's also possible," Martin said.

The ringing phone brought Traveler awake in the middle of the night. He switched on the light to check his father's bed. Martin hadn't returned from Moroni.

"Damn," Traveler muttered, wide awake with the adrenaline triggered by a two A.M. call.

"Yes," he said warily.

"Mo, it's me, Claire."

He expelled the breath he'd been holding. "Where are you?"

"Listen to me, Moroni. My life's in danger."

"Give me some credit, for God's sake. I'm not falling for your craziness again."

She'd disappeared several times since he'd known her, twice when they were still living together. Each time she'd phoned, demanding rescue from nonexistent enemies.

"Claire, I'm going to hang up."

"For the love of Jesus, don't. I beg you. I made a mistake this time, with these people. They're dangerous. They're—" A sharp cry of pain cut off whatever she'd been about to say.

Traveler shook his head. He'd been through that ploy before, a cry for help that had damn near gotten him killed.

"Goodbye, Claire."

"Just do what they tell you, Moroni. That's all I ask."

"Tell me about the boy. The boy you named after me. That's all I want from you."

"Goddammit!" she shouted. "It's me they've got."

"I'm sorry," he said. "Goodbye."

He was about to hang up when another voice broke in. "We read about you in the paper, Mr. Traveler." The voice, though distorted, sounded distinctly feminine. The cadence was slow and precise, like someone reading an unfamiliar script. "About how you took on three men to help your girlfriend here. We appreciate that kind of loyalty."

"Stupidity is more like it," he said.

"Make no mistake, Mr. Traveler. We expect the same kind of consideration from you now."

He sighed. "I hope she's paid you in advance."

"Money isn't important to us."

"Of course not. You want me to come riding to her rescue, like the cavalry."

"No indeed, Mr. Traveler. Exactly the opposite. We want you to go home."

In the background Claire screamed. It was real enough to raise gooseflesh.

"I'm not buying it," he said and hung up.

He was thinking about walking over to the office to unplug the switchboard when the phone rang again.

He grabbed the receiver. "Give it a rest, Claire. You're not going to sucker me again."

"Leave Wasatch by morning," the voice said. "Otherwise we'll cut her throat."

"Go ahead," he said, refusing to play her sick games for once, paying her back with a dose of her own medicine, as all the while a part of him wanted to rush after her one more time.

Traveler was still trying to get back to sleep when someone knocked on the cabin door. He squinted against the dawn light.

"Who is it?"

"Me," Martin said.

"Use your key."

Martin rattled the door. "The chain's on."

A mosquito slipped through the crack and came after Traveler, humming in his ear as he stumbled across the room to unlatch the chain. "Your widow must have thrown you out of bed early."

"She got a call," Martin said.

"So did I." Traveler headed back to bed. "Claire at two A.M. The same old thing. She wanted me to rescue her again."

"What did you say?"

Martin's tone of voice stopped Traveler dead in his

tracks. He swung around but Martin's face, backlit by the
dawn, was in shadow and impossible to read. "I told her I
was through playing games."

Martin sighed. "You know how it is with these small
towns. They've got their own kind of jungle telegraph.
That's why the sheriff here knew where to reach me in Moroni. He was the one who asked me to come see you."

Traveler's fingers were shaking by the time they found the
lamp switch. Martin's despairing face looked ashen in the
bright light.

"We can stop looking for Claire," he said.

Traveler sat heavily on the bed.

"She's dead, Mo. Her throat's been cut."

"The sheriff's waiting down the road about a half mile," Martin said. "The Wasatch Cafe. He wants to talk to you."

Traveler had his eyes closed, thinking about Claire. The only image that came to mind was of her sitting in the front row of the courthouse, her lips tucked into the hint of a smile that said *I win no matter what.*

"That's where I had my run-in with Ellis Nibley's sons," he said.

"Could they have done this?"

Traveler replayed the phone call in his mind. "They're not that devious. Besides, it was a woman. I'm sure of it."

"Did you lock the Jeep last night?"

"Yes."

"Then whoever did it came here last night, broke into the car and hot-wired it. Did you hear anything?"

"Firemen were coming and going all night."

"We can ask around. We might get lucky and find a witness."

"Why take the Jeep?" Traveler asked, though his suspicions were already making him queasy.

"You don't want to know."

"I'd rather hear it from you and be prepared."

Martin sighed. "They wanted to make sure you got the message. She's tied to the hood the way hunters transport deer."

Traveler tasted bile. The Nibleys were hunters. "It's my fault she's dead."

His father's mouth opened and closed. If words had come out, Traveler couldn't hear them. The throbbing pulse inside his head was suddenly too loud.

He bent over at the waist, bracing his hands against his thighs, and concentrated on breathing. Traveler squeezed shut his eyes. When he opened them again, Martin was rubbing his neck muscles.

"Take it easy," Martin said. "Let me do the talking."

The words, though understandable, sounded as if they were echoing along a tunnel. "Let me tell you a story about your mother. What do you say?"

Traveler didn't speak.

"I went away to war a bridegroom. When I came back I'd gained a son and lost a wife. It was the happiest day of my life until I made the mistake of asking her why she'd been unfaithful. 'You left me alone, didn't you?' she said. 'With a son to raise. It's your fault I had to seek help elsewhere.' She cried then and told me her tears were for me, that I was the guilty one, the one who had to be forgiven. And you know what? She made me feel guilty, for Christ's sake. Fool that I was. So don't you start thinking that way. Learn from my mistakes."

Traveler swallowed sharply. "Easy for you to say."

"Is it?"

"I understand what you're trying to tell me," Traveler said, knowing that his own presence was a reminder of Kary's betrayal. "But I should have listened more carefully. I should have known Claire's cries for help were real."

"How many times has she called you? Half a dozen? More? Each time it was the same. You said yourself she was a great actress on the phone."

Traveler straightened up, making it impossible for Martin, a foot shorter, to keep up the massage.

"I'm surprised the sheriff didn't come here in person," Traveler said.

"You'd have to be a fool to tie a body to your own car. He knows that. Besides which, there's a volunteer deputy waiting outside. From the looks of him, he must have been a volunteer fireman last night."

"Does the sheriff have any idea who did it?"

Martin shook his head. "He said it wouldn't have happened if we hadn't shown up."

"He's right," Traveler said. Claire's face came to him, the way he'd seen her the first time. He lurched into the bathroom and held on to the sink while it filled with cold water. When he plunged his face into it, he wanted to rinse away his memory. Rid himself of the momentary relief he'd felt when Martin said Claire was dead. When he knew she could no longer torment him. But nothing changed. His guilt was intact.

"She cried wolf too many times," Martin said.

Traveler heard her cry for help again.

"Jesus," he sputtered into the water. He rose up, shaking himself.

Martin handed him a towel.

"It was a woman's voice on the phone this time. That should have alerted me. Claire would never use another woman to play one of her games. She didn't get on with them."

"Just like your mother."

Traveler pounded his fist against the image of himself in

the mirror. Killing Claire didn't make sense. Unless the suicides were murder.

"Why run me out of town?" he said. "When I don't know anything?"

"You know something. You just don't realize it."

Traveler hit the mirror again, cracking it this time.

"I know that look of yours. Violence won't get you anywhere, unless you're beating on the right person, of course."

"I loved her once," Traveler said.

"And now?"

Traveler shook his head. There was no way he could explain his obsession with her.

Someone knocked on the door.

"That'll be the deputy," Martin said.

The deputy, still wearing protective fire clothing, hitched his gun belt and opened the passenger door on the sheriff's cruiser. His only piece of uniform, other than the belt, was a Stetson like the one the sheriff wore. Martin slid onto the front seat while Traveler got in back, feeling like a prisoner behind the grillwork shield. Norma Beasley, with Baby Joe in her arms, stepped out of the motel's office to watch them on their way.

The sun hadn't been up more than half an hour, but the temperature was already in the eighties. The smell of smoke had disappeared, along with the wind. But smoke was still rising from the mountain peaks, reminding Traveler of volcanoes on the verge of eruption. Flames were visible, too, making him feel as if he were already in hell.

"We want you to identify the body." The deputy started the engine.

"I did that already," Martin said.

"Sheriff Hickman wants confirmation."

Martin half turned and reached a finger through the grille as if to touch his son. "I wanted to spare you that."

"I never saw anything like it before," the deputy went on, his Adam's apple fluttering. "Laid out like that, it's . . ." He swallowed whatever he'd been about to say.

As the cruiser passed by the office, Mrs. Beasley took hold of one of Baby Joe's arms and waved it. Perhaps it was the fanning motion, perhaps it was Traveler's imagination, but the smell of the woman's rose toilet water suddenly engulfed him. As always, the smell of roses reminded him of his cousin, Orson, and the last time they'd played catch together in front of Grandfather Ned Payson's house. For some reason Traveler's mother had put an end to the outing, driving him home while he protested all the way that there was still enough light left to keep on playing. Without him, Orson had begun a game of catch with himself, bouncing the tennis ball off the front steps. A wild ricochet had sent him into the street from between parked cars. The driver, Traveler remembered his mother saying later, didn't even have time to put on his brakes.

That night he'd heard his parents arguing.

"A funeral is no place for a boy his age," Martin said.

"He has to be there. It's expected."

"By whom?"

"Everybody," Kary said, her tone giving no leeway.

"It's best to remember someone the way they were," Martin responded. "That way they're never really dead."

When the time came, Traveler had tried to resist. But his mother dragged him by the hand into Grandfather Ned's living room where the coffin, surrounded by roses, lay across sawhorses draped in black. Kary had lifted him up to kiss Orson goodbye. He had makeup on and smelled just like the roses.

The deputy pulled onto the shoulder of the road, bypassing the Wasatch Cafe's gravel lot, and killed the engine. He nodded at Traveler to get out, but his hands stayed on the steering wheel, gripping hard enough to show he had no intention of following.

The Jeep was parked to one side of the cafe, near the phone booth. A green plastic tarpaulin had been thrown across the car's hood. The mound beneath it looked too small to be Claire. The sheriff and a woman Traveler didn't recognize were standing nearby.

"I'll go with you," Martin said.

Part of Traveler wanted to tell the sheriff to go to hell, wanted to walk away and remember Claire as she was in memory. Another part wanted to be alone with her one last time.

He took a deep breath and got out. "I'd better do this alone."

"I understand," Martin said. "I'll wait for you."

Sheriff Hickman detached himself from the woman and joined Traveler next to the tarp.

"I'm sorry," Hickman said. "Your father told me how close you were to her."

Traveler sucked air through clenched teeth.

"I've taken photos of everything," the sheriff added. "Doc Gourley is on his way over from Ephraim. We can't move her until he gets here. So if you'd rather wait till he gets her cleaned up, I understand."

"If you're giving me an option, why send the deputy?"

"You're a pro. You know it's never a good idea to waste time."

Traveler glanced at the lady bystander, who was trying not to stare at him but couldn't help herself.

"We couldn't spare any men off the fire line," the sheriff explained. "The only man left in town besides me and my

deputy—and he's only with me temporarily—is Ellis Nibley.
He wouldn't be of any use to us anyway because of his griev-
ing, that and the town wanting to keep the general store
open. So Pearl McConkie is here representing her husband,
the bishop, and the council. She came straight over from
fixing breakfast at the Relief Society."

To Traveler, she looked interchangeable with the two
previous Mrs. McConkies he'd met. "What is she, a witness
in case I confess?"

Hickman shrugged.

"What about the Nibley boys?" Traveler asked.

"Everybody in town knows about your run-in with those
two, so I checked on them first thing. If someone was trying
to make them look guilty, it was a mistake. They were accounted for all night, what with fire fighting and the bishop's
prayer meetings."

Traveler sighed. "Let's get it over with."

Hickman turned back the tarpaulin far enough to expose
Claire's head and neck.

"Christ." Traveler nodded and swallowed hard, thankful
for an empty stomach. "That's Claire." He jerked away, closing his eyes, trying to recall Claire alive. But her gaping
throat was like a blinding afterburn.

A hand touched his arm. Without looking he knew it
was his father.

"There's no blood," Traveler said.

"She wasn't killed here," the sheriff answered.

Traveler opened his eyes to bright sunlight, cool by comparison to the burning image inside his head. The tarp was
back in place.

Pressure increased on his arm. "We can talk about details
later," Martin said, pulling steadily in the direction of the
cafe.

"Pearl volunteered to fix us breakfast," Hickman said. "I,
for one, could use something hot to drink."

"Where was she killed?" Traveler asked.

"There's no need for you to see it."

Traveler glared.

"Suit yourself." The sheriff led the way out behind the cafe, where he pointed to a length of frayed rope hanging from the limb of a cottonwood tree. Directly beneath the rope the darkened ground shimmered with flies. "The way I figure it—"

Traveler cut him off. "I get the picture."

She'd been strung up by her feet and butchered. The Mormon way, blood atonement to pay for her sins.

"I warned you once before," Hickman said. "Now I'm asking you again. Leave Wasatch."

Martin shook his head. "'We, and each of us, covenant and promise that we will not reveal any of the secrets of this, the first token of the Aaronic priesthood, with its accompanying name, sign, or penalty. Should we do so, we agree that our throats be cut from ear to ear and our tongues torn out by their roots.'"

Traveler swallowed, aware of his own tongue. His father was quoting from the temple ritual of endowment, the time when secret oaths and names were bestowed on the faithful, when the laws of blood atonement were laid down.

"The killer has to be someone who knows church ritual," Traveler said.

"Since you both seem to know it so well, maybe I ought to arrest you. It would at least get the Relief Society off my back."

"Maybe so," Traveler said.

For the first time, he truly understood blood atonement. Understood why Mormons still swore temple oaths against the federal government, against those they blamed for the murder of their first prophet, Joseph Smith. Understood why Brigham Young sanctioned killing, under the guise of saving sinners, in order to survive his enemies. But unlike Brigham, Traveler had no intention of sending anyone to heaven. He was going to send Claire's killers straight to hell, personally.

Traveler stared at the plate of half-eaten scrambled eggs the bishop's wife had fixed. Continuing hunger added to his guilt. That and his memory of the sudden sense of relief he'd felt when he realized he was off the hook forever. That Claire would never again torment him.

He sipped Mormon tea—hot water and milk—and watched Martin pile marmalade onto a piece of toast. The sheriff was outside dealing with Dr. Gourley, who'd arrived from Ephraim.

"May I get you two something else?" Mrs. McConkie asked. She'd been fussing over Traveler and his father for the last ten minutes. She no longer looked embarrassed, though Traveler had caught her staring at him in the mirror a few times.

"We're fine," Martin said with his mouth full.

"I'll leave you men alone, then, and go do the dishes." Once she'd disappeared through the swinging door into the kitchen, Martin groaned. "God, how I need a cup of real, honest-to-God, sinful coffee."

"Ask her."

Martin shook his head. "To hell with it. I'll get my jolt from the Coke machine back at the motel."

Traveler had tried that yesterday, but found it stocked only with sin-free 7-Up. "I'll make us some coffee myself."

Martin waved his half-eaten toast in the general direction of the kitchen door. "You'll hurt her feelings."

"The cafe wouldn't have coffeepots if this town wasn't full of Jack-Mormons." Traveler spun off his stool and moved around the counter. From there, he saw that Dr. Gourley had finished his examination and was supervising the loading of the body into the ambulance that had accompanied him from the neighboring town.

Martin must have seen the same thing reflected in the mirror behind the counter. "I wonder when we'll get the Jeep back?"

An Ephraim police car, driven by an officer equipped with a fingerprint kit, had come with the ambulance.

Traveler opened the cupboard above the hot water urn and found a small jar of instant coffee. "If this were Salt Lake, we wouldn't see it for days."

"You shouldn't have told Hickman that Claire was a Gentile."

"I told him the truth, that she no longer went to church."

"In rural Utah, that's like saying she was in league with the devil."

Traveler fixed two cups of strong coffee and handed one to his father. "Some relative will baptize her after the fact soon enough."

"Don't get any ideas like that when *I'm* gone," Martin said after his first sip. "I don't want you or anybody else standing in a baptismal font for me."

Traveler tested the coffee and made a face. "I want you to take the Ford and drive back to Salt Lake."

"That will leave you stranded until they're finished with the Jeep."

Traveler mixed Mormon tea into his coffee. "I'll rent a car or buy one if I have to. I want you to locate Claire's parents. Find out anything you can about the Bennion family. For one thing, I want to know why they left Claire behind when they moved away from Moroni."

"You heard Dora Neff. Claire didn't want to leave her high school."

"Claire never graduated from high school. She told me so herself."

"Nice try, Mo. But I know you too well. I can see your mind working. You're thinking that whoever tried to use Claire against you might make the same move on me. So you send your old fart of a father to Salt Lake and out of harm's way."

"Salt Lake's a loose end," Traveler said.

"Sure."

"Okay, for Christ's sake. I admit it. It's a hell of a lot easier if I don't have to worry about your back and mine too."

"Bullshit. I'll be covering your back."

Pans banged in the kitchen, probably a protest against such profanity.

When Traveler reached across the counter to grab his father's hand, Martin pretended to misread the gesture. "Keep your hands off my toast, damn it." Pushing the plate ahead of him, he scooted over a stool. "We've got work to do, like going over your plans for the day so I can back you up."

Traveler didn't argue. There was no use. He knew his father.

"You didn't happen to bring a gun with you, did you, Dad?"

"Hell, no. I thought this was a suicide. They don't usually shoot back."

"I'll tell that to our client. He's first on my agenda for the day."

"Besides," Martin said, "I don't figure we'll need a gun. It's been my experience that someone who kills women doesn't have the guts to go up against a man."

"Thinking like that can get you killed."

Martin snorted. "If I thought there was any real danger I'd tell you about your mother before it's too late."

"For Christ's sake." For years Traveler had been trying to get the truth out of Martin, including the name of Kary's lover, Traveler's father. "Tell me about it so I won't have to worry for once."

"Sperm doesn't think. It just reacts. That's why upbringing is all that counts."

Sheriff Nibley opened the cafe's front door. "You can have your car back if you want it. My advice is for both of you to go home."

"I thought we were suspects," Martin said.

"I know where to find you."

"We'll be at Ellis Nibley's," Martin said. "To start with."

Nibley's General Store, like just about everything else in Wasatch, was on Main Street. It was a squat, single-story building with a new aluminum facade that failed to hide the original oolite around the edges of the door and along the side walls. A flat, corrugated metal roof projected over the sidewalk. From it hung a rusted Coca-Cola sign.

A nearly vacant lot, its cement island a reminder of a long-gone service station, separated Nibley's from the town library.

Traveler parked the Jeep—hosed off but still showing stains—across the street, in front of McConkie's Feed and Seed. His father got out, nodded, and settled against the fender to wait.

The door to the Feed and Seed stood wide open. The lights were on inside, doing their best to fight off a midmorning twilight created by the smoky sky. Even so, the store looked deserted. So did every place else in town.

Traveler crossed the street, his shoes making sucking sounds on the hot, sticky asphalt. He was scraping his soles on the sidewalk when he noticed the faces inside pressed against the front window. Women's faces, distorted by grimy glass. He nodded at them. They retreated.

A bell tinkled when he opened Nibley's door. The women had clustered in front of a long counter that ran the length of the store. All were staring at Traveler. Behind them stood Ellis Nibley. He was on tiptoe to see over them, shaking his head at Traveler, a signal of some kind, most likely that he didn't want to talk in front of witnesses. Traveler had half expected him to be at the fire, despite the bishop wanting the general store to stay open.

At Traveler's approach, the women filed past him toward the door. The last in line paused to say, "I'm Sarah Mc-Conkie. Mrs. Bishop McConkie. I run the Feed and Seed across the street."

Traveler smiled. He'd lost count of the bishop's polygamous adherence to God's word, as translated by Joe Smith. Utah was full of such men. Some said polygamists numbered as many as forty thousand. But then Smith's revelation had given the faithful no leeway. Either they practiced polygamy or they were denied the kingdom of heaven. The modern-day church had counter-revelations in place, put there to pacify the federal government back in the 1890s. But those steadfast to Joe Smith, Black Bishops like McConkie, chose to ignore such revisionist doctrine.

"The other ladies," she went on, "have made me their spokeswoman. We want you to know what we think of you and your father being here."

"My father is not part of my investigation."

"We never had a killing in Wasatch before you came."

From the doorway, the other women nodded in unison.

"The dead woman was your friend," Mrs. McConkie said. "The word is that you lived with her."

"How do you know that?"

"You were read about in the Salt Lake paper. She took you to court." Disgust warped her face. "She didn't belong here and you don't either."

"She was born in Moroni," he said.

"She went away a sinner, we know that much. She came back no different. If you hadn't come here, she would have died somewhere else and we'd all be free of it."

She pointed a finger at Nibley. "You share the blame on this, Ellis, as you do with Melba."

With that, she pushed past Traveler and herded the other women out onto the sidewalk. There they paused, looking back and forth between the mountains and Traveler. No doubt they blamed him for the fire, too.

"She's right," Nibley said. "I should never have hired you. First, my son gets his ribs stove in. Now this. You warned me to leave well enough alone. I should have listened."

"Your sons attacked me, not the other way around."

"I know that, but it doesn't change what happened. You're free to leave if you want."

"I can't," Traveler said. "I think you understand that. There's something wrong in this town. Whatever it is, it was here before I arrived. Now, let me ask you again. Are you certain your wife killed herself?"

The man's face, already painful to look at, lost all color. His groping fingers found the cash register stool behind him. He collapsed onto it. "She can't have been murdered, Mr. Traveler. No one around here would do such a thing."

"Tell me again what happened."

His hands grabbed hold of the sides of the stool. "She left a note. In her own handwriting. I must have told you that already."

Traveler nodded.

"She did it in the bathroom." Nibley's voice cracked.

"The door was locked. I had to break it down. Sheriff Hickman said there was no doubt at all."

"Yet you hired me."

Tears started from Nibley's eyes. "Like I told you before, I wanted to know why. What I really wanted, I think, was to have you tell me I wasn't to blame. But I was wrong, like the good book says. 'Oh, this unbelieving and stiff-necked generation—mine anger is kindled against them.' I am guilty of being stiff-necked. I know it. Even so, I still want to know the truth, Mr. Traveler. I must know if my sins are to blame, if I've broken our seal of eternity together."

Traveler stared at the front window. The women stared back.

Traveler nodded at them before turning back to Nibley. "Do you have a copy of the note?"

"I have a copy."

"May I see it?"

He reached behind him to switch on more lights, a row of green-shaded bulbs that ran down the store's center aisle. Dust-laden light pooled beneath them.

"I can't help," Traveler said, "if you keep things back."

Nibley hung his head and dug out his wallet, the one his son had made for him in shop class, and extracted a tightly folded paper. Carefully and gently, as if his wife's touch extended to the Xerox, he smoothed the paper out on the countertop. His eyes tracked the lines before he turned the note around so Traveler could read it.

The handwriting was neat and precise. *Forgive me, my dearest. I'm sorry.* At the bottom of the page in a loose, deteriorating script, as if an afterthought induced by tranquilizers, was written *Josiah 13:22.*

When Traveler looked up, Nibley sighed and reached beneath the counter for a pocket-size copy of *The Book of Mormon.* Without a word, he handed it to Traveler, who quickly found the reference and read it out loud. "'Thou shalt not commit adultery.'"

Traveler stared at his client until the man squirmed.

Nibley grabbed the book, slapped it down on the counter, placed one hand on it, and raised the other. "May I be damned to hell if I'm lying. As far as I know, my wife was faithful to me. I have no reason to think it wasn't suicide. I promise you, I had nothing to do with her death."

"Were there other women in your life?"

"Not even once," he said, his hand still on the book.

"Unfortunately, your wife can't speak for herself."

"She was a God-fearing woman, Mr. Traveler. The pills must have affected her mind. Or maybe she made a mistake about the quotation."

Over the years, Traveler had heard a lot of husbands say the same thing about infidelity. Some believed what they said, others didn't.

Nibley looked like one of the believers. It was the believers who killed their wives when they discovered ugly truths.

Traveler said, "Why didn't you tell me there'd been a second suicide here in town?"

"Joe Sutton. Doctor Joe? It didn't have anything to do with my wife."

"But he was your wife's doctor. You said so in my office."

"Here in Wasatch he was everybody's family doctor."

"Are you certain that he killed himself?"

Nibley blinked. "He had cancer. Everybody knows that. Talk to Mrs. Joe if you don't believe me. She was his nurse, too."

TWENTY-EIGHT

Following Nibley's directions, Traveler headed east on Main, turned left at the first intersection, Brigham Street, and then continued three blocks to Heber Avenue. At Heber, he turned right again, one block to Kimball Street. All the while, his father watched the rearview mirror.

Ashes from the fire were falling from the sky like blackened snow. Traveler rolled down the window and reached out with cupped palm. The ash eluded him.

The Sutton house was on the corner of Heber and Kimball. It was an older home, possibly from the 1880s, set amid Depression-era bungalows half its size. Traveler parked in front.

Martin got out first and stood, hands on hips, admiring the house. "The Gothic Revival style," he said as soon as Traveler joined him, "unless I'm mistaken. Which I'm not."

It had a gabled roof with three dormer windows opening onto a balcony that ran the entire length of the house. Beneath the balcony was a long front porch.

The yard was big, with setbacks on both sides, one accommodating a garage, the other an abandoned outhouse. The driveway was cluttered with junk—bicycles, parts of a car, and what looked like a doctor's examination table, complete with stirrups for female patients.

Seeing it made Traveler shudder. Once, when making love to Claire, with her bucking beneath him like a wild animal, he'd said, "I feel like I need stirrups to stay on."

Though on the brink of orgasm she'd rolled away from him.

"What's wrong?"

"A horse ran away with me once with my feet caught in the stirrups," she answered breathlessly. "I promised myself never to put my foot in a stirrup again."

Traveler forced his mind away from the memory. "This had to be the finest house in town at one time."

Martin shook his head. "That'll be the bishop's. You can count on it." With a sigh, he took out his handkerchief and handed it to his son. "Wipe your face. You look like a Catholic on Ash Wednesday."

Traveler checked his hands. They, too, were sooty. "I keep hearing that phone call from Claire."

"You missed a spot."

Traveler gave back the handkerchief and started up the cement walk toward the front door.

"Do you want me to come with you?" Martin called after him.

Traveler came back to say, "You wrote the rules. Two of us might intimidate the woman."

"I hate that, when you quote me to get your own way." Martin fought a losing battle against a smile before returning to the car.

A woman wearing a starched white uniform answered the door. She was the same one he'd seen at the Co-op, the one who'd been working silently on the quilt. She'd been introduced to him as Jessie, not Mrs. Joe.

"It took you a long time to get around to me," she said and invited him in.

They entered a parlor that reminded him of a doctor's waiting room. Long benches lined opposite walls, facing a coffee table filled with magazines staggered one on top of the other so that their titles showed. A massive fireplace of blue enameled brick, with a matching mantel lined with picture frames, took up the remaining wall.

Mrs. Joe sat on one bench and pointed him to the other.

She looked to be sixty, gray haired, buxom, not yet fat, somewhere in the transition from mother to grandmother. Her trim legs, sheathed in white nylon, rustled when she crossed them. She smiled when she caught him admiring them. A well-practiced smile, he thought. One to reassure the patients while waiting for their appointment with Doctor Joe.

"Mrs. Sutton—"

"Please," she interrupted, "call me Mrs. Joe. Everybody else does."

"They called you Jessie at the Co-op."

Her enigmatic smile reminded him of Claire. "They say you're named after our Angel Moroni."

"I was named after my father."

She nodded as if that was to be expected. "So was my husband. Named for his father who was named for *his* father. Suttons have been living in this house since 1876. My husband had his first office right here in this room. In those days we couldn't afford a place downtown. Oh, I know this house is the biggest on the block and looks expensive. But it's impossible to heat in the winter, and a monstrosity when it comes to plumbing and wiring. If Doctor Joe hadn't been the only doctor in town, his patients would have gone somewhere else in the wintertime just to keep from getting goose pimples during their physicals."

He smiled, hoping she'd get around to the subject of her husband's death without prompting from him.

She smoothed her skirt, which crackled from heavy starch. "'I know we're working out of our home,' Doctor Joe used to say, 'but that's no reason not to wear a fresh uniform every day.' Even after he passed, I never got out of the habit. I don't go into the office these days, but see no reason to waste perfectly good clothing."

Rather than face her intense stare, he rose and went to the fireplace, intending to look at the photographs. But most of the frames were empty. Those that weren't showed Jessie Sutton as a young girl.

"Why don't we go in the kitchen?" she said. "Being in here always makes me feel so formal. My desk was right here in front of that door, guarding the way to my husband's examination room. I always had to sit up straight and look professional." She tried to slump but the straight-backed bench prevented her. "See what I mean?"

The kitchen had a white tile floor, matching countertops, and glass-front cabinets showing elegant china alongside jelly glasses and chipped, everyday crockery. It all gleamed.

"Coffee?" she said. When he looked surprised, she added, "It's not really coffee. It's coffee-flavored Postum with no caffeine. Do you think it a sin to pretend you're drinking coffee?"

"Not unless it makes you feel guilty."

She smiled. "That's what I think. Cream and sugar?"

"Please."

To keep from making a face while drinking the Postum, he wandered around the kitchen, coming to a stop in front of a stack of casserole dishes.

"The neighbors brought them in when Doctor Joe passed on," she explained. "I can't bring myself to return them yet. It would be . . . I don't know. An end to things."

"Tell me about your husband?"

"You don't fool me," she said. "But why not? I've got to talk about him sometime."

Momentarily, she busied herself washing their cups. "You have to understand about us, Mr. Traveler. We were married in the temple in Manti. Hands were laid upon us. We were anointed with oil. Our secret names were bestowed."

She reached under the neck of her uniform and drew out a delicate gold chain from which hung an inch-long glass phial. "This contains consecrated oil, Mr. Traveler, from that temple. I keep it with me always in case a miracle is needed."

Traveler's mother had kept her supply of healing oil in the medicine cabinet, next to the Mercurochrome.

"I'm not a school-trained nurse," she said. "But I do have a gift. Doctor Joe used to say that I was better even than Cynthia Odell. Of course she and her husband are being shunned these days." She shook her head. "I can hear Doctor Joe now. 'You're my insurance,' he'd say. 'My sure cure for cases beyond my university education.'"

Her eyes shone. For a moment, Traveler thought she might be putting him on. Then he dismissed the idea. He'd met few Mormons willing to joke about their faith.

"I wish I could use my power to help Ellis Nibley. I know the poor man hired you. There's nothing I can do or say to give him comfort, though I want you to know that I've done my best. I've even gone through Doctor Joe's files which, strictly speaking, are confidential. Even so, I'll tell you what I found. Nothing. Nothing in writing to show why Melba would take her own life."

"And your husband?" Traveler said gently.

"Doctor Joe had cancer. It was just a matter of time. The pain would have gotten worse."

Had she laid hands upon him too? he wondered. And anointed him with oil?

"Could I see those records?" he said. "Since all concerned are dead."

"Not even I was allowed to see them when Doctor Joe 1
was alive. I only read them after he passed on." 4
"A judge might order you to give me those records." 9
"You're not the first to threaten me. Sheriff Hickman
came here asking for them too. I'll tell you what I told him.
Doctor Joe's records are nothing but ash."

"You burned them?"

"I had them cremated with him."

Martin took one look at his son's face when he got in the car and started singing a song he'd sometimes used as a defense against his wife's sharp tongue. He used it still in times of stress. "'You can bring Peg with a wooden leg, but don't bring Lulu.'"

Traveler started the engine. "I think Mrs. Joe was holding something back. I had to walk out of there to keep from wringing it out of her."

"'You can bring Sy with a glass eye, but don't bring Lulu. I'll bring her myself.'"

"Goddammit. I keep hearing Claire begging for help. It makes me want to kill somebody."

Martin took a deep breath and let it out slowly. "She made you feel guilty when she was alive, and she's still doing it now. Your mother had the same effect on me."

"I remember her telling me once that she didn't trust men who were fathers. She said they didn't take care of their children properly. When I asked about her own father, she said he was dead. She said her whole family was dead as far as she was concerned."

Without warning, Traveler let go of the steering wheel and hugged his father so hard he couldn't squirm. "That makes me realize how lucky I am."

"Let me go, for Christ's sake. I can't breathe."

Traveler released his grip. "I just wanted to say it for once."

"I taught you better than that. Keep your mind on your work and don't get emotional. Where to now?"

"Back to Shirley Colton. Maybe now, with Claire dead, she'll tell me what the hell is going on with the State Medical Board."

"Don't count on Saints telling a Gentile anything."

Traveler tapped himself on the head with a knuckle. "You're right. I'm not thinking. Since the Saints don't trust us, we'll talk to the town Gentile."

Two minutes later he parked in front of the library, a converted single-story brick house old enough to have been built before Main Street was strictly commercial. A sign on the glass storm door said the library was open three days a week, and today wasn't one of them.

"I'll wait for you out here," Martin said. "If you take too long, I'll be up the street at the dinette getting a cup of coffee."

Traveler walked to the door and pressed his face against the glass. Hope Leary, whom he'd met at the Relief Society, was sitting at a desk on the far side of the room. At the sound of his knock, she lurched out of her chair. One hand went to her throat. For a moment, she looked too frightened to move.

"I didn't mean to startle you," he said as soon as she came to the door. He stepped back to give her room.

"I'm not used to having people arrive on off days," she

said. "They're not great readers here in Wasatch, so it's slim pickings even when we're open. But I don't think you're here to check out a book."

She was a small-boned woman with black hair, blue eyes, and a skim-milk complexion. Black Irish came to mind.

"I need an ally," he said.

"I have to live here after you're gone, Mr. Traveler."

"One Gentile to another."

"I'm too old to go looking for another job."

"A woman's been killed."

She studied him closely. "Wasatch being what it is, I'm sure your presence here is no longer a secret, so you might as well come inside."

The room smelled of book mold and lilac perfume. She led him to one of two oak reading tables. When he sat down, lemon furniture polish overwhelmed the other scents.

She folded her hands on the tabletop and stared at them, waiting for him to begin.

"I'm sure you know what's happened. Someone I knew has been murdered."

She spoke without looking up. "Did you love her?"

"Once."

"I'm sorry."

"Her death brings the count to three here in Wasatch."

"Surely the first two were suicides?"

"Then why kill Claire Bennion when I show up?"

She raised her head to examine him again. "I didn't know Melba Nibley well. Or Doctor Joe either for that matter. I was his patient only once, when I had the flu. Neither one of them were great readers."

"What do you know about an investigation by the State Medical Board?"

Her hands jumped from the table to her breast. "Me?"

"The first woman I talked to in Wasatch thought I'd been sent here by the board."

"Who was that?"

"Shirley Colton. She also told me there were others in town who had written to the board. Were you among them?"

"I'm almost as much an outsider as you are."

"You must know what's going on."

"I know a lot of things, Mr. Traveler. Mostly it's gossip that ought to be ignored. When it comes to something really important, people don't confide in me, not directly anyway."

"Does that mean you won't help me, or can't?"

"Let me tell you something about Wasatch." She paused, tilting her head as if gathering her thoughts. "If you walked up Main Street right now, what would you see? Women. They're running this town right now. Even Sheriff Hickman would be on the fire line if it hadn't been for you and your Claire. You know what that says, don't you? Except in times of emergency, the women of Wasatch are invisible. They're at home tending children, cooking, doing housework, or anything else too menial for their husbands to bother with."

"Not everybody is a Black Bishop like McConkie," Traveler said.

"Don't make that mistake. His wives are no different from any other woman in this town. Like all of us, they don't exist without their husbands. If their husband is important, be he a bishop or sheriff or mayor, they're important too."

"And you?"

"I'm not married and I'm a Catholic to boot. I dispense books, that's all. Like a Coke machine. The whole state's like that, a men's club run by the church."

"That doesn't help me."

"Given such a situation, what would it mean for a woman, or a group of women, to take action on their own? What would be important enough to make them do such a thing?"

"Like writing to the medical board?"

"I'm afraid that's all I know, Mr. Traveler. If what you

say is true, then something made them so desperate they went against their husbands and acted on their own."

"But you don't know what it could have been?"

She sighed. "I've known Shirley Colton a long time. Most of the others too. Well enough to read the suffering on their faces."

"What others?"

"You're the detective. I'm only a librarian. If I had a husband, I wouldn't even be that. I'd be his wife."

It was late afternoon by the time Traveler found Shirley Colton in the basement of the Co-op, where she and a dozen other women were taking inventory of the ward's stockpile of food, clothing, and fuel. He knew the same thing was probably being done in storm cellars all over town. Church doctrine requires that each family have its own cache of supplies, enough to last the year of Armageddon, which only the Latter-day Saints would survive.

"I'd like to speak to you alone," he told her.

The other women left their tasks to form a loose circle around her. Some carried clipboards, others mops and brooms.

"You had no business coming here, opening old wounds," she said.

Whatever they were, they couldn't be as bad as Claire's wounds. He was about to say as much when the women tightened their circle around her. Their movements were as precise as some childhood game set to rhyming chants. He lost sight of her.

"I need your help," he said.

As a group, the women edged forward, forcing him back toward the door through which he'd come.

"A woman has been murdered," he said.

They kept coming.

"Mutilated in the Mormon way."

They hesitated.

"I loved her once."

"There are worse things than death," one of the women said.

"Hellfire," another said.

"Hell here on earth," Shirley Colton added.

"Please." Traveler went up on tiptoe to make eye contact with her. "Tell me why you wrote to the State Medical Board."

Her head shook. Others picked up the movement.

"Was it about Doctor Joe?"

"I'm sorry you've lost someone close. I know how you feel. But I can't talk about it anymore."

They began moving toward him again, brandishing their mops and brooms.

Backing up, he said, "I'm not leaving Wasatch until I find her killer."

"This is our town." A woman emerged from the group and signaled for a halt. "I'm Vera McConkie, the bishop's wife. I think I can speak for everyone here."

She paused, waiting for confirmation. Silence gave it to her. "If the men were here, they'd run you out of town. For once, we'll have to do their work."

With that, she signaled a charge. He turned and fled, taking the cellar stairs three at a time. They weren't more than ten feet behind him when he reached the Co-op's main room. There, he had space enough to sprint.

Martin saw him coming and reached across the front seat
to open the car door. Traveler threw himself inside, with
barely time enough to lock the door before the women surrounded the Jeep. They began pounding on the windows.

"They say they're the weaker sex," Martin said, starting
the engine and revving it.

"Be careful for God's sake."

"Maybe you'd like to drive?"

"Just get us out of here."

Slowly Martin backed away from the curb. Despite the
Jeep's movement, the women continued to attack from all
sides.

Martin braked, straightened the wheels, and shifted into
drive. "And to think you wanted me out of the way in Salt
Lake. Who would have come to your rescue if I hadn't been
here?"

Space cleared around the Jeep. Immediately, a rock
cracked the windshield.

"We certainly have a way with women, you and I," Martin said.

More rocks pelted the car.

Traveler found Shirley Colton in the crowd. She had a
rock in her hand and tears in her eyes. "Get us out of here
before one of them gets hurt," he said.

"Sometimes I think you're too innocent to be a detective." Martin eased ahead, one foot on the accelerator, one
on the brake in case he had to stop quickly. After half a
block, the women broke off their attack.

"Where to?" Martin said.

Feeling exhausted, Traveler slumped in the seat. "Head
out of town. We'll find someplace to eat along the highway.
By the time it's dark, it ought to be safe enough to come
back to the motel."

"I think we'd better take turns sleeping tonight in case
those women decide to set their husbands on us."

Traveler was already awake when someone knocked on the bungalow door shortly after sunrise the next morning. He waved his father into the bathroom before answering it, keeping the night chain in place. Only one woman greeted him. Mrs. Beasley was standing on the doorstep with her baby in one arm, a folded newspaper in the other.

"They just delivered the Ephraim *Enterprise*," she said. The sun was striking her and the child in the face, making her black hair look darker than ever while turning the boy's red hair into a fiery halo.

"I thought you'd want to see it." She thrust it through the opening. As soon as he took hold of it, she turned and walked away.

He retreated inside, suddenly aware that he was wearing only his shorts, and closed the door. The paper was folded open to an inside page. An obituary notice had been circled in ink.

Our beloved daughter, Claire Sue Bennion, 32, has been called home.

Born September 23, 1958, in Moroni, Utah, to Duane and Naomi Bennion, she attended Moroni High School and was an active member of the local ward of the LDS church. She was president of her Sunday school class.

She is survived by her parents and by her brothers and sisters, Lamar, Harold, Stanley, Virginia, Joyce, and Martha.

Traveler sat heavily on the bed. He tried to reread the obit but his eyes wouldn't focus.

Martin, still in his pajamas, took the paper and read it for himself. When he finished he rolled it tightly and started chasing mosquitoes, leaving swat marks of newsprint on the wall whenever he missed.

"Got ya," he said finally. "Look at that. The sucker was full of blood. Our blood."

"I never thought of Claire going to Sunday school," Traveler said.

"They say female mosquitoes are the worst," Martin said. "They bite with a vengeance."

"All those brothers and sisters and yet she always gave me the feeling she was alone in the world."

Breathing hard, Martin collapsed onto the other twin bed. "What gets me worst," he panted, "is when they whine in your ear."

"I wonder how the newspaper got the information. From the sheriff, do you think? Or her parents?"

"It could have been Dora Neff," Martin said.

Traveler rubbed his eyes until they stung. "I'm willing to

bet that woman knows more about Claire than she's told us."
He blinked away the tears he'd created.

"Women always keep back something. That's the only
way they can be sure you stay interested."

"Come on. We can get breakfast on the way to Moroni."

Overgrown weeds on either side of Highway 116 had kept
Traveler from spotting the signs on his first trip to Moroni.
But as a passenger he didn't have to watch the road.

WHISKERS LONG

MADE SAMSON STRONG

BUT SAMSON'S GAL

SHE DONE

Traveler read it out to his father.

"Well?" Martin said. "What's the rest of it?"

"The last part's missing."

Martin snorted. "Samson's not in *The Book of Mormon*,
you know." He took one hand off the wheel to scratch at the
day-old growth on his chin. "If you ask me, the Mormon
prophets took a page out of Samson's book. Especially Brigham Young. No Burma-Shave for him. He kept his hair,
wore a beard, and got himself twenty-seven wives."

"You forgot to shave," Traveler said.

"Maybe Dora Neff will do it for me."

When they arrived, Dora Neff took one look at them and
said, "You men don't look like you've eaten in days."

"We had coffee and a doughnut down the road," Martin
said.

"That's no way to keep your health. You two come into
my kitchen this very minute and I'll fix you something de-
cent. You're in for a treat if you like eggs. I keep my own
chickens out back. They came through with half a dozen this

morning. We'll add a little fresh cream from my neighbor's cow and whip up some scrambled eggs. I'll toast some of my homemade bread, too. How does that sound?"

Traveler decided not to ask questions until after they'd eaten, in case she took their prying personally and threw them out. But he needn't have worried. She immediately brought up the subject of Claire herself.

"I did my crying for that child years ago." Her red eyes said otherwise. "I did my best for her, too, Lord knows. But in my bones I knew she'd come to a bad end. Though I never imagined anything as bad as this."

She turned away from them to stir eggs on a Kelvinator range not much younger than she was.

Traveler started to speak but his father beat him to it. "We're going after Claire's killer, you know that, don't you, Dora?"

Her shoulders rose and fell. "I know a missionary look when I see one. I knew you didn't come all this way just to see me." She brushed at her hair. "What is it you want?"

"Anything you can think of that might help us."

"I don't know who killed her. That's for sure. It couldn't have been one of the Saints, though. I feel that in my bones. Certainly not anybody from around these parts."

"You said Claire got a call when she was here. Was it from a man or a woman?"

She half-turned and waved a spatula at them. "I didn't answer the phone. But I had the impression that it was a man. In high school, the boys were always calling Claire. Sometimes they'd camp out on my front porch waiting for her to come home. Boy crazy, she was. But nothing went on in my house. I always saw to that. I chaperoned her properly. Now let me get these eggs on the table before they get cold."

Martin didn't speak again until he was on his second helping. "What was Claire like when she first came to live with you?"

Dora didn't answer immediately, but concentrated instead on her coffee-flavored Postum. When she finished the cup she made another for herself. Neither Traveler nor his father had touched theirs.

"I'm sorry you don't like it," she said, eyeing their cups. "Claire wouldn't drink Postum either. She preferred Ovaltine. Even that was a sin, or so her father said. He wasn't the brightest man, that's for sure. Not when it came to religion. Or raising children either, for that matter."

She fussed with her apron. The cloth, which had a hand-stitched beehive on the front, looked stiff and unused. "Do you remember your Word of Wisdom? 'Strong drinks are not for the belly, but for the washing of your bodies. And again, tobacco is not for the body, neither for the belly. And again, hot drinks are not for the body or belly.' Poor old Duane Bennion. He thought that meant hot from the fire and nobody could tell him otherwise. So there wasn't so much as Mormon tea served in his house. I tell you this to show you what kind of background Claire came from. What she was fighting by the time she moved in with me. Mind you, I consider myself a religious woman. But there are limits to what God expects of us. At least, that's the way I see it. In any case, I wasn't the only one who thought Duane was an extremist. Nobody would hire the man, because he kept getting into arguments. Finally, he decided to go looking for work in Salt Lake. At least, that was the story his wife gave out."

Martin nodded encouragement. Traveler closed his eyes and tried to remember Claire as he'd first met her. But all he could see were the terrible wounds.

"Claire didn't come to me straight off. She went to stay with her Grandma Frieda first. Frieda Bennion on her father's side, rest her soul. After a month Frieda came to me and said she couldn't keep her. She said she was too old to have her life turned upside down by a fifteen-year-old. There was more to it than that, naturally, but I didn't find out about it until Claire moved in with me. She was a handful, I can tell you. Boy crazy like I said before."

Traveler interrupted. "I still don't understand why her family left her behind here in Moroni."

Dora stared him in the eye. "I don't like speaking ill of the dead. Even now, after what's happened, I wouldn't tell you if I thought that would be the end of it. If the dead would be left in peace. But too many people around here like gossiping about fallen Saints like Claire. Even after she's been away from us for so many years."

She paused, patting herself on the breastbone to catch her breath. By the time she started speaking again, tears were spilling from her eyes. "Occasionally Naomi, Claire's mother, would send me a few dollars to help pay expenses. Whatever money she could earn that her husband didn't know about. The way that child was going through clothes, I had a hard time making ends meet. I was a widow even then, you see, with only a small pension. Of course, after a couple of months the clothes couldn't hide Claire's problem. She was pregnant, you see. When I found out, I tried to get help from her father. But he said she had sinned and that he wanted nothing more to do with her. He said she was lost as far as he was concerned. He forbid his wife or children to see her again."

My God, Traveler thought. No wonder Claire had played games with him, pretending to be lost in hopes that he, that anyone, would come looking for her.

"I tried to find out who the father was," Dora said. "Not that I would have made her marry some high school boy. But somebody should have helped pay the bills. In any case, Claire wouldn't tell me. She said I wouldn't believe her."

The woman wiped her eyes on the edge of her apron. "She tried telling her father in the beginning, she'd said, when she first knew she was pregnant. But he beat her for telling lies."

"What lies?" Traveler said.

"All I know is what she told me. That her father locked her up in the root cellar and made her memorize her sin from *The Book of Mormon.*"

She held up a hand before Traveler could speak. "That child used to go around the house repeating it over and over. I learned it by heart, too. 'O the wise, and the learned, and the rich, that are puffed up in the pride of their hearts, and all those who preach false doctrines, and all those who commit whoredoms, and pervert the right way of the Lord, wo, wo, wo be unto them, said the Lord God Almighty, for they shall be thrust down to hell.'"

"The poor girl," Martin said.

"What happened to the baby?" Traveler said.

"She had a boy. He was adopted. I can't say by who. It wouldn't be fair. Doctor Joe over in Wasatch helped me make the arrangements."

"Where is the child now?" Martin asked.

Dora sighed deeply. "He died, poor thing, when he was only a baby."

"She had another child," Traveler said. "One she named after me. Did she tell you about that?"

Her eyes fixed on him, condemning him. "Claire couldn't help herself with men. But you, Mr. Traveler, you should have known better. You should have helped her when there was still time."

On the way back, Traveler stopped along the road to search for the missing Burma-Shave signs. All he found was empty beer cans, some of them predating aluminum, and enough cigarette butts to sin for every man, woman, and child in Moroni.

While Traveler rummaged along the gravel shoulder, Martin walked up the road to the first of the signs still standing. As he walked back toward the Jeep, he shouted out the surviving slogans one by one. "Whiskers long . . . made Samson strong . . . but Samson's gal . . . she done . . . him wrong . . . Burma-Shave."

"That's great," Traveler said. "You found them."

Martin shook his head and slid into the passenger seat. "I remembered them from Sunday drives with your mother. I was her Samson and you were Claire's. She had to destroy you, just as Delilah did, though all the time she was hoping you'd be strong enough to beat her at her own game."

"Christ." Traveler climbed in behind the wheel. "It's more important than ever that you go back to Salt Lake and find Moroni Traveler the Third."

"I'm not sure he exists."

"The postmortem ought to tell us."

Martin sighed. "Claire didn't want to be a mother. She was looking for a father, one who wouldn't abandon her. You."

"She was the one who kept running away."

"She had to keep testing your loyalty, didn't she?"

Traveler laid a hand on Martin's arm. "I can't imagine anything worse than being abandoned by your father."

"You won't get rid of me that easily," Martin said. "I plan on staying here with you."

"We know Claire didn't have the child with her here. That means the answers, if there are any, have to be in Salt Lake."

"Drive," Martin said.

Traveler swung out onto the highway and headed east toward Wasatch. A smoky haze obscured the mountainous plateau for miles in either direction. The closer they got to town the thicker the smoke became. By the time they were driving up Main Street, visibility was down to half a block. Breathing the hundred-degree air was like smoking one of Barney Chester's cigars.

"We ought to pick up some of those filters you can wear over your nose." Martin coughed to prove his point.

"If you ask me, they're more trouble than they're worth," Traveler said. Even so, he U-turned and parked in front of the drugstore. The wind had picked up, he noticed, enough to add dust to the smoke.

Martin stood on the sidewalk, hands on hips, admiring Odell's Drug Store. "Pure Utah Outback. That limestone looks like it was cut yesterday."

Traveler was about to go inside when he noticed the

building's second story. Three identical windows ran across
it. All were dirty; all had their shades drawn. The center window contained faded gold lettering: JOSIAH SUTTON, M.D.

"I've remembered something," Traveler said. "Claire had a thing about doctors."

Martin glanced at his son before shifting his gaze to the upper floor.

"We'd gone to Liberty Park once to ride the merry-go-round. She said she wanted to catch the brass ring and win a prize. Only they didn't have a ring."

Traveler closed his eyes and saw her hair flying out behind her like a mane. Saw her toss her head in joy. Heard her laugh.

"She said there was a ring to be grabbed just the same. That it was invisible to everyone else."

She'd grinned and licked her lips like a child tasting cotton candy.

"We were sitting side by side. Claire had the outside horse. Each time we went around she'd grab at the invisible ring."

Each miss made her laugh all the harder.

"Finally she was hanging by one hand and stretching so far out the attendant yelled at her. But not soon enough. Her wrist hit one of the wooden support beams. It hurt like hell, but she wouldn't cry. Instead, she kept saying, 'I almost had it.' She only started crying when it swelled so badly I told her she'd have to see a doctor. She got hysterical then. Said she wouldn't see a doctor, no matter what, that she didn't care if she had a crooked wrist the rest of her life."

He'd carried her to one of the benches from which nonriding mothers watched their children. *"Please, Moroni, I'm begging you. No doctor. I hate them."* All the while the attendant kept wringing his hands and saying he was insured. *"You've got to do it,"* Traveler had told her, knowing from experience how intense the pain of a broken bone would be once shock had worn off. *"For me if nothing else."*

"It took me half the night, pleading, threatening even, before I finally got her to an emergency room. Even then, she wouldn't be left alone. I had to stay right with her, holding her good hand like a child the whole time she was being treated."

"There are times when we all feel like that," Martin said. "When we need to hold on to someone."

"It was more than that. You would understand if you'd seen her eyes. She was terrified."

"We all have bogeymen from our childhood."

Traveler stared at the gold lettering. "What would happen if you went back to Salt Lake and camped outside the State Medical Board?"

"You know better than that. We don't have the clout to force those damned doctors to talk to us. Besides, I told you before. You're not getting rid of me."

Traveler's chin sank onto his chest. "That doesn't leave me any choice."

Martin squinted at him. "I don't like the sound of that."

"I'll have to ask Willis Tanner for a favor."

"Then God help us."

Martin sat at the soda fountain, drinking a chocolate phosphate under the close scrutiny of Cynthia Odell, while Traveler made his call from the phone booth at the back of Odell's Drug Store. He dialed Willis Tanner's private number, the one, according to Willis, that the church kept totally secure and that was good any time of the day or night.

A recorded voice asked for his access code.

At that point Traveler was supposed to punch in his social security number, but the phone had only a dial. The message was repeated once more before a live operator came on the line. Sounding surly, she asked for his number. He could hear her entering the touch-tone beeps at her end.

The line sound changed. No doubt a church computer was sorting through his life. TRAVELER, MORONI. FALLEN ANGEL.

"Is that you, Mo?" Tanner said.

"What does your computer screen say?"

Tanner laughed. "That's you, all right. I heard you were down south."

"In Wasatch."

"I think Hal McConkie's the bishop there."

"Even you can't be that good, Willis, not with thousands of bishops across the state."

"Aren't computers wonderful?"

More likely it was Church Security at work, a system run with religious fervor by ex-FBI agents.

"I need a favor," Traveler said.

"What are friends for?"

Traveler imagined Tanner's squint-eyed smile.

"I need access to records at the State Medical Board."

"What would I get in return?"

Traveler didn't hesitate. "Anything you want."

Tanner whistled. After that, there was silence on the line.

Traveler, sweating at the thought of what price Tanner might extract, opened the door to fan air into the booth. Until now, he'd always been careful to keep their accounts even, since owing Tanner was like owing the church.

"I'll be damned," Tanner said.

Traveler heard something that could have been Tanner jumping for joy.

"I'm looking out at your namesake, Mo. I think I hear his trumpet sounding."

Tanner's office, high up in the old Hotel Utah building, looked out on the temple across the street. His floor was only one below the penthouse, the official residence of the church president. Both were well below the golden statue of the Angel Moroni.

"'Before the arm of the Lord shall fall, an angel shall sound his trump,'" Traveler said, a Sunday school lesson remembered.

"There's hope for you yet, Mo. Hold on, while I record your promise of payment."

"You have my word, Willis."

"That's good enough for me. You know that. But . . ." In the pause that followed, there was no sound, no click, no beep, nothing to indicate a recording device. "Go ahead. We're all set."

Traveler took a deep breath. "Claire's dead."

"I heard. I'm sorry."

"But not sorry enough for a favor without strings?"

"I'm not a free agent," Tanner said.

"She was murdered."

"I heard that too."

"In the Mormon way," Traveler added.

"You're talking ancient history, Mo. Oaths that no longer have meaning. Now what is it you need exactly?"

"Letters were written to the State Medical Board from women here in Wasatch. I need to know what's in them."

"That's a civil matter. It doesn't come under church jurisdiction. Surely you understand that."

"What I understand, Willis, is that nothing is beyond your jurisdiction if you so choose."

"I don't see how I can help you, not without something more concrete."

"You sound like you know what's going on here already," Traveler said.

"You know me, Mo."

"All right. On tape and for the record. You do this for me and I, Moroni Traveler, will owe you one. Payable on demand."

"Give me your phone number and I'll get back to you."

Traveler hesitated. Martin was slumped over the fountain's counter, looking tired and in need of rest. But if they went back to the motel, the old-fashioned switchboard offered no security whatsoever.

"How soon, Willis?"

"Let's say an hour. There could be a lot of records to go through."

What the hell, Traveler thought. An eavesdropper on the line might make his work easier by spreading the word and stirring up things.

He gave Tanner the number of the Sleep-Well Motel.

An hour to the minute Tanner called back. He sounded subdued. "I've got the file in my hand, but I've been advised to keep names out of our conversation."

"Are you alone?"

"Except for my tape recorder, which is definitely off. I want no record of this conversation."

Martin, who was listening in as best he could without an extension, mouthed, "Don't trust him."

Traveler shrugged. "All right, Willis. Tell me what you've got."

"Eighteen letters written over a period of twenty years. Eight of them were recent, apparently mailed together as a mass protest."

"Am I to assume that all complaints are against Doctor Joe, Dr. Sutton?"

"I told you, Mo. No names."

"Have you forgotten our deal? As of now, I owe you one."

"I love having you in debt to me, Mo. But when I saw the file I almost backed out of the deal. This is very confidential information."

"I need to know about Shirley Colton's letter."

"No names, remember. I'll read you one that's representative of the others."

"Hers?"

"I didn't say that."

"I'm listening."

Tanner cleared his throat.

> "Dear Sirs, I am writing to request an investigation of Doctor X, whose conduct toward me and my family is nothing short of criminal. I have made a similar request of the sheriff here in town, as have other patients who are writing to you at the same time. Every time I visit Doctor X's, whether for a cold or anything else, he always insists on giving me a pelvic examination. His practice is to prescribe a tranquilizer first, then make me wait in his office until the drug takes effect. He does it, he says, to quiet my nerves. I end up feeling so groggy his nurse has to help me up onto the examination table and into the stirrups. But she leaves the room when the doctor comes in. He drapes me in such a way that I can't see what he's doing when he dilates me. However, I recently had occasion to visit another doctor, a female specialist. Her examination convinced me that Doctor X uses his penis instead of a dilator. That makes him a rapist."

Tanner paused for breath. "There's more, but I can't see how it would help you. In any case, I won't bother reading the other letters, since they say pretty much the same thing."

"You say these complaints go back twenty years?"

"That's right."

"What action has the medical board taken during that time?"

"None."

"What the hell's going on?"

"I asked the same question, Mo. You know doctors. They protect their own. As the letters trickled in over the years, they put it down to female hysteria. When the last eight letters arrived together, there was some talk of an investigation. But there's no point in pursuing that now with Doctor X dead."

"That's very convenient."

"My sentiments exactly, Mo."

Traveler and his father were digesting lunch at the Main Street Dinette, along with the information supplied by Willis Tanner, when Sheriff Hickman arrived. Father and son nudged one another. Without a word, Traveler slid one stool to the left so Hickman could squeeze in between them.

"What'll it be, Sheriff?" the woman behind the counter said.

"Vera, I'm surprised to see you open."

"You know the bishop when it comes to business." She winked good-naturedly. "Besides, I put in my time earlier at the Relief Society."

"This is Vera," the sheriff said. "Bishop McConkie's wife. She makes the best apple pie in town."

"We've met," Traveler said. "Mrs. McConkie ran me out of the Co-op."

The woman smiled.

The sheriff said, "Church business is not for outsiders. I told you that once before."

Mrs. McConkie handed the sheriff a slice of pie. If Traveler hadn't been looking at Hickman, he wouldn't have caught the signal. But the woman picked it up. "If you want anything else, I'll be in the back. Just yell." She left them alone.

Hickman nodded and went to work on his pie, while Traveler drank coffee and wondered if the sheriff knew about the call from Willis Tanner.

"I'm the only man in town not fighting the fire," Hickman said, pushing away his empty plate. "Ellis Nibley excepted, poor man. I would be on the line, too, if we didn't have strangers in town."

"Somehow I don't think you came here to give us a fire report," Traveler said.

Hickman smiled, but his eyes were as cold as those Traveler had seen in photographs of the sheriff's gun-fighting ancestor. "I've checked with some people I know in Salt Lake. They tell me you're a dangerous man, Traveler."

"Are you sure you talked to the right people?" Martin said. "My son and I have the same name."

Hickman licked pie crumbs from his mustache. "We've had a wind shift. The fire has circled around and is now burning toward the road leading out of town. If it reaches the road, Wasatch will be cut off from the outside world. When that happens I can't be responsible for you two."

"We'll get by," Traveler said.

"Living around here isn't easy. Us locals have learned how to survive."

Martin said, "I was just telling my son that I wasn't leaving until we get what we came for."

"I think you'd better tell us about Dr. Sutton," Traveler said.

With a grunt, Hickman spun off the counter stool. "That man brought most of us around here into this world. He saw a lot of us out, too, with compassion and kindness."

"There are people in this town who say otherwise." Traveler swiveled around to face him.

"I underestimated you," Hickman said. "Or maybe I overestimated my neighbors. I didn't expect them to tell you the local gossip. But that's all it is. Malicious gossip."

Hickman poked a finger against Traveler's chest. "A sheriff can't act on rumors, not when someone's reputation is at stake. Someone like Doctor Joe."

"Letters were written to the State Medical Board," Traveler said. "I don't call that rumor."

"A man in my position needs proof, corroborating witnesses."

"For God's sake," Martin said. "Did you even bother to investigate?"

"I asked the Doc about them once. He laughed and said that's the chance every doctor takes when he examines female patients."

Traveler and Martin exchanged quick, confirming glances. Willis Tanner's information had been on the mark.

Hickman shrugged. "I figured you already knew some women were complaining. According to the Doc, ladies tend to fantasize about their doctors. It's their way, he said, of cheating on their husbands without any actual risks."

"And you let it go at that?"

"I was waiting to see what action the state board took."

"Sure," Martin said. "It's always safer to wait."

"The men in this town elect me," Hickman said.

"And the women?" Traveler said.

"Don't try laying your guilt on me. I didn't get your girlfriend killed. If you ask me, you did that by being here."

The sheriff pointed his finger at Traveler's chest again. Traveler was about to bat it away when his father spoke. "The doctor killed himself before any action could be taken. That ought to tell you something, Sheriff."

"The man had cancer," the sheriff said. "It's as simple as

that. On top of everything else, he was devastated when he learned there was to be a formal hearing on the charges."

"Now we're getting to it," Traveler said. "What hearing?"

Hickman took off his hat and rubbed his bald head. "My own son wouldn't be alive today if it wasn't for Doctor Joe. The boy swallowed a toy and started choking. I wasn't home. My wife called Doctor Joe. He dropped everything and came running."

Traveler had been watching the sheriff's face as he spoke. The man's expression was devout. Yet Hickman had to know what twenty written complaints in a town the size of Wasatch meant. Most likely there were a hell of a lot more women who hadn't had the guts to come forward. Especially with something as personal as sexual misconduct.

"Describe Doctor Joe for me," Traveler said.

"What do you mean?"

"Was he handsome?"

"I never thought about it much."

"Start now."

Hickman tugged at the drooping tips of his mustache. After a moment he gave that up to scratch his sideburns. "Like I told you before, he was a saint. He even had a halo."

"What the hell is that supposed to mean?"

"His red hair. I always envied him that."

"Jesus Christ," Traveler muttered. He'd seen that kind of halo before. On the Beasleys' little boy.

Traveler parked in front of the Sleep-Well's office, hoping that Mrs. Beasley had been eavesdropping on his earlier conversation with Willis Tanner. That way, at least, she'd be expecting the personal questions he was about to ask.

Martin stepped out on the passenger side of the Jeep, pushed his fists into the small of his back, and groaned. "I'm getting too old for this kind of thing."

Through the window, Traveler saw Mrs. Beasley sitting in front of her switchboard. A tattered Hire's decal obscured her face.

She turned to greet them the moment they came through the door. Her dress, a shiny green fabric with plate-sized flowers the color of dying gardenias, fit like a raincoat. Baby Joe was perched on her lap, his face streaked where tears had cleaned away the grime. Mrs. Beasley's face powder showed similar inroads.

"Sheriff Mahonri called a few minutes ago," she said. "He thought you'd be coming to see me."

"Is that why you look upset?" Traveler said.

"Baby Joe's cutting a tooth and kept me up last night. Besides which, I don't feel safe here anymore. Not after what happened to that woman. Seeing your car pull in just now brings it all back. It's no wonder Baby Joe's cranky."

"That call I got this morning," Traveler said, "did you happen to catch where it came from?"

"What do you think I do, listen in? Besides"—she pointed at the switchboard where every cord was plugged into a different socket—"we're keeping the lines open as long as the fire's burning. You know that."

Martin sighed.

Traveler said, "We need your help, Mrs. Beasley."

"You don't have to call me Mrs. Norma's fine by me."

Traveler smiled. "Norma, we're trying to find out more about Doctor Joe."

"Is that what all this is about? From the way the sheriff sounded on the phone, you'd think the world was coming to an end. Well, I'm the person to talk to, all right. I owe Doctor Joe everything. But then I guess I told you that already." She nuzzled her baby's neck, making him giggle. "Baby Joe's named for him."

"If I remember correctly," Traveler said, speaking softly, calmly, "you told me you were childless for years before the doctor helped you."

She kissed Baby Joe on the lips. "That's right."

"This is personal, I know, but can you tell me what procedures he took?"

Her face flushed almost as red as her baby's hair.

"I wouldn't ask," he rushed to say, "but I'm trying to find some way of comforting Ellis Nibley."

"I don't see what my medical problem has to do with that." She deposited her child in the playpen. "You've been listening to Shirley Colton, haven't you? Well I, for one, wouldn't have that woman in my house. She ought to be shunned just like the Odells."

Martin said, "I'm afraid it's more complicated than that."

"You don't have to be cagey with me. I know Shirley's got a bunch of old ewe muttons on her side. Malicious women spreading lies like that about Doctor Joe. It's a sin, if you ask me."

"Has Shirley Colton talked to you personally?" Martin asked.

"I wouldn't listen if she tried."

"Then how do you know what's being said about the doctor?"

Mrs. Beasley put a hand to her cheek, then slowly dragged her fingernails across it, leaving white scratch marks behind. "I heard it from Mrs. Joe. That woman has enough troubles without something like this."

"When was that?" Traveler asked gently.

"Right after Melba Nibley killed herself. I think Mrs. Joe went around talking to just about everyone in town. If you ask me, she was looking for the same thing you are, a reason why it happened. If I know Mrs. Joe, she probably felt responsible, her being the doctor's nurse and all."

Traveler slumped against the lowboy counter, trying to make himself smaller, less threatening. "How many other women like yourself did Doctor Joe help?"

Mrs. Beasley rubbed her cheek, where welts were rising to replace the scratches.

Martin went to the window and pretended to look out. "We'd rather not bother his widow if we don't have to."

When Mrs. Beasley caught her breath and straightened her shoulders, Traveler thought they'd lost her. Thought that she was about to throw them out.

"All right. I'll do it for Mrs. Joe. But you've got to understand something first. I've never talked to my husband about this. Never."

She scooped up Baby Joe, hugging him to her, and returned to her chair in front of the switchboard. She kept her back to them while she spoke. "Doctor Joe ran tests on both me and Nat. Finally, he said it was a dilation problem. That . . . that the sperm wasn't getting where it was supposed to. He said he'd have to enlarge me gradually, using a special instrument. I think he called it a dilator. Anyway, I had to go to his office once a week until I finally became pregnant. Is that what you want to know?"

"Was Mrs. Joe present during the examinations?"

Mrs. Beasley rocked her baby in her arms. "She was usually too busy. She had to give shots, keep records, send out the bills, things like that."

"What did the dilator feel like?" Traveler asked.

The back of Mrs. Beasley's neck flushed.

Traveler racked his brain for euphemisms, for some way to keep her as a willing witness. "Did it feel like your husband?"

The woman twitched. Baby Joe began to whine.

"Like when you make love," he amended.

"Is that what the ewe muttons are saying?"

Traveler looked at his father and mouthed, *What do I say?* Martin shook his head.

After a long silence, Mrs. Beasley said, "I don't remember."

"You went every week. You couldn't have forgotten."

"I was always nervous, you know, embarrassed when Doctor Joe examined me. He gave me tranquilizers to take just before I came into his office. They worked wonders, because I'd practically fall asleep right there on the table."

"Both you and your husband have brown hair."

"I'd already decided to name my baby after Doctor Joe, long before I saw the color of his hair."

"What did your husband say?"

She swung around, her eyes bright with tears. "Don't go listening to him either. I told him the same thing I'll tell you. Our prayers were answered. That's all that counts."

"I have a feeling we're going to need a woman with us from now on," Traveler told his father once they were outside. "Why don't you drive to Moroni and see if you can recruit Mrs. Neff?"

"What makes you think she'll want to get mixed up in this?"

"It's something the druggist's wife, Cynthia Odell, said to me. She said physical exams were required for all high school students around here, and how Melba reacted to hers."

"That was a long time ago."

"Exactly. But Doctor Joe practiced medicine in this town a long time. On top of that, Wasatch is the closest town to Moroni. My guess is that he worked the schools there too. If that's the case, I think Mrs. Neff will want to be here."

"I'll do my best," Martin said.

"Don't say anything more than you have to. That way she'll be our independent witness."

"I'll use my charm on her."

Once Martin was on his way in the Ford, Traveler took the Jeep and headed for the fire line. The command post was set up in the foothills at the head of Grant Avenue, near where it turned into Dority Canyon Road. Three large open-sided tents, army surplus judging by their khaki color, had been erected in a row along one shoulder of the road. They provided shade for the half dozen or so men lying on cots inside. A smaller tent, with first aid crosses made of duct tape, stood some distance from the other three, as if the druggist, Enos Odell, were being shunned even here.

Cars and tractors were parked on the other side of the road. Traveler pulled the Jeep in at the end of the line of vehicles. From there he could see that the fire was burning in a half circle around the town. If the circle closed, Wasatch would be cut off from the main highway just as the sheriff had said.

Traveler found Odell alone in the first aid tent, sitting on a canvas cot staring at a medicine chest marked with red crosses. The man's white smock, buttoned up despite the heat, had turned gray with soot.

At Traveler's entrance into the tent, the druggist looked up expectantly as if hoping for a patient. Odell was a big man, almost as big as Traveler, with flab instead of muscle. He was sweating profusely, yet still exuded that old-fashioned drugstore smell.

"Remember me?" Traveler said.

Odell nodded.

"I never did get an answer from you about Melba Nibley's tranquilizer prescription."

"I don't give out medical information, especially when it concerns Doctor Joe. He was a friend."

"I'm not accusing him of anything. I'd just like to know why Mrs. Nibley needed that kind of drug. Was she a nervous woman?"

"Everybody's nervous at one time or another."

"Nerves would have to be chronic, I'd imagine, before a doctor could prescribe such a drug in good conscience."

"Doctor Joe was a saint. Everybody says so."

"How many pills did you give her?"

"Whatever the prescription called for."

"For Christ's sake. A woman's been murdered."

Odell ducked his head as if expecting violence against him. "I didn't know *her.*"

Traveler clenched his fists so hard they trembled. He ached to hit someone. "Well, I did, goddammit."

"I'm sorry, but I don't see that one death has anything to do with the other."

"Answer my questions. That's all I ask."

"I can't release personal information."

"Mrs. Nibley is dead. I work for her husband. Nobody's going to sue you."

The druggist shook his head, keeping it up until Traveler ran out of patience. He grabbed the man's smock, popping a button, and jerked him to his feet. The man cringed, waiting to be hit, but still didn't speak.

Frustrated, Traveler released him. "Thank you for your help."

He turned abruptly and left the tent, feeling the need to shun the man like everyone else. He was about to enter the main command post when Bishop McConkie, a folding camp chair in one hand, a walkie-talkie in the other, intercepted him.

"We don't have time for you, Traveler. If you don't leave the area, I'll have your car bulldozed off the road."

"You need my help."

"I've already called for backup," McConkie said, misunderstanding Traveler. "Fire fighters are here from Ephraim and Manti. Their orders are to keep the road open behind us."

"Worse things can happen to a town than fire. Like murder."

"Take another look around you. If this thing keeps burning the way it is now, we'll start losing houses in another quarter of a mile. Clem Dority has already lost some outbuildings. Now get out of here."

"I have to talk to Nat Beasley."

"Don't try telling me he's a killer," the bishop said.

"He has information I need."

"All I have to do is shout for help. A dozen men will come over here and make you leave. Or worse."

Traveler shook his head. "You have three deaths on your hands already. Two so-called suicides and Claire Bennion. You didn't see her, but I did, tied to the front of my car like a hunting trophy. So you're not going to stop me, unless you're willing to kill me."

"What do you mean *so-called?*"

"I arrive in town looking for a way to help Ellis Nibley cope with his wife's death. The next thing you know someone wants to stop me badly enough to kidnap Claire Bennion and kill her. Does that make sense if all we're talking about is suicide?"

McConkie pointed in the direction of the nearest flames. "We're already paying for our sins."

"I know about the letters to the medical board," Traveler said. "Did Melba Nibley write one, too? Or has that been hushed up?"

McConkie collapsed onto the camp chair he'd been holding. The canvas sling creaked beneath his dead weight. "Dear God. I prayed that would never come to light."

Traveler dropped into a crouch. Logic said a bishop, particularly a man with gossip-gathering wives all over town, would know just about everything that went on. "How many women complained about Doctor Joe?"

McConkie sighed deeply, got a lungful of smoke, and

started coughing. By the time he had recovered, his voice sounded hoarse. "For every woman who said he was a devil, an equal number claimed Doctor Joe was a saint. I kept hoping the medical board would act and take it out of my hands."

"And did they?"

"Every time I contacted them, they said they were investigating. They've been saying that for years. Finally, we had no choice. We excommunicated him."

"Are you telling me that he was still practicing medicine after that?"

"What more could we do?"

Any number of things occurred to Traveler, but he kept them to himself. "His suicide was very convenient. It took care of your problem."

For a moment the bishop's line-free face showed cracks. Traveler shifted his weight, expecting trouble. But all the bishop did was raise the walkie-talkie to his mouth and order Beasley to report to the command post.

After that, McConkie rearranged his chair so that he was facing east toward the heart of the fire. They waited in silence, watching flames explode in the tops of pine trees not more than two hundred yards away.

"Here he is," McConkie said finally. He stood, folding the chair under his arm.

The figure stumbling toward them, in hard hat and overalls, bore little resemblance to the motel owner Traveler remembered. He was soot-covered and weary, like a soldier coming out of battle. He sagged onto the ground as soon as he reached the bishop.

"I want you to give Mr. Traveler five minutes of your time. After that, Nat, come find me."

"I'm expected back at my post."

"We'll need to talk first." McConkie patted the man on the shoulder and walked away.

Traveler eased himself into a cross-legged position facing
Beasley. "I just came from the motel. Your wife told me everything."

Beasley removed his hard hat, laid it beside him, and
knuckled his eyes.

"I know about the letters to the medical board," Traveler
said to prime the man, to make him think that there was no
longer a need to hide anything.

"What do you want from me?" Beasley said after a while.

"I'm an adopted child myself," Traveler said, stretching
the point. "My father and I don't share the same blood. That
bothered me for a long time, when I was too young to know
better. I did some research on genetics in those days. But you
know what my father said? It's not the genes that count, it's
your upbringing."

"I've done a little checking myself. It's not impossible for
dark-haired parents to have a redheaded child."

"What are the odds?"

Beasley swung a fist at Traveler but missed. Momentum
and exhaustion left him flat on his face in the dirt.

Traveler started to help him, then thought better of it.
"You heard the bishop. I'm here with his permission. He expects you to answer my questions."

"It would kill my wife if this got out."

"I'm after a killer, not gossip."

Beasley righted himself. "All right, for God's sake. Why
shouldn't I tell you? Anybody with eyes could see it. At first,
my wife said it was just temporary, him having red hair. All
babies are blonds, she said. But instead of getting darker, it
just got redder. So what do you expect? Of course I got suspicious. Who wouldn't? Is that what you want to hear?"

Traveler looked away from the man's tortured eyes and
kept quiet.

"For Norma's sake, I pretended he was my son."

"He is your son."

"I even let her name him Baby Joe. But I think she must have known too, down deep, that he wasn't mine. I could see it in her face sometimes. A sadness. I kept telling myself that it wasn't like she'd been unfaithful. Hell, she didn't even know what was happening to her during those exams. Doctor Joe was clever that way. He'd been treating people around here for twenty years. Twenty years of getting away with it. There are still some who don't believe it. I heard them at the Bishop's Court. Women swearing on *The Book of Mormon* that the man was a regular saint."

"What kind of women still believe in him?" Traveler asked.

"I know what you're getting at, that the man must have left the old and ugly untouched."

Traveler thought about Norma Beasley. She wasn't a pretty woman, but then he hadn't seen her before the pregnancy.

Tears mixed with soot on Beasley's cheeks. He unbuttoned his shirt and used the front of his Mormon undergarment to dry his face. "It wasn't like that. He preyed on the shy ones, the women who wouldn't understand what he was doing. Or wouldn't admit it. You must think I'm a fool. That we're all ignorant fools. What we are is small-town people. It's as simple as that. We're not suspicious of folks, especially our friends and neighbors."

"Did you ever ask your wife what went on in the doctor's office?"

"Norma's too shy to talk to me about things like that."

Too shy or too smart, Traveler thought. The need for a child may have clouded her judgment. Or perhaps she was afraid of what her husband might do if all doubt was removed.

"Even at the Relief Society, where the women chatter all day long, my Norma's a quiet one," Beasley said. "Ask anybody."

Traveler decided to bring his thoughts out in the open. "Do you think Doctor Joe could have been murdered?"

"You're looking at me, aren't you? Well, I don't blame you. After the bishop's court, I wanted to kill him myself."

"Is that when he was excommunicated?"

"You're damned right. I wanted to strap him onto that table of his, put his feet in those stirrups and cut his balls off. So did a lot of others around here. But the bishop wouldn't let us. 'Let God deal with him,' he said. 'He's done enough to our town already without turning us into killers.'"

Beasley ground his teeth. "That's easy for the bishop to say, turn your cheek and all that. As for me, I hope the bastard's burning in hell."

"Was he a religious man?"

Beasley ignored the question. "I can't understand people sometimes. Especially those who believe he was railroaded by a few hysterical women. I mean, for God's sake. Damn near every woman in town was on that table of his at one time or another."

"Your wife said he prescribed tranquilizers before her examinations?"

"Strong stuff, let me tell you. She'd take one an hour before seeing him and be walking around like a zombie by appointment time. I didn't dare let her drive by herself."

"I don't get it," Traveler said. "Why did it take so long for someone to realize what was happening?"

"It was strange how we found out. Shirley Colton was visiting relatives in Salt Lake and took sick and— Damn, I shouldn't be telling you this. I probably wouldn't be, either, if I wasn't so tired." He shuddered. "Sick and tired of everything that's been going on."

Traveler waited, knowing a wrong word or expression could end the interview.

"Like I was saying," Beasley continued, "Shirley was sick, some kind of female complaint, and went to see one of those woman doctors. When she gave Shirley a pelvic, Shirley couldn't believe how quick and easy it was. Nothing like what Doctor Joe put her through. So she asked the woman about it, and saw the proper instruments for herself. And that's when she realized what Doctor Joe had been dilating her with all those years."

"She told you this herself?"

"It was Lew, her husband, who spilled the beans to the rest of us. That was the night I kept him from murdering Doctor Joe Sutton."

"What held you back?"

"He hanged himself. He didn't have any choice once we found out about him."

Traveler let that go for the time being. "What did Melba Nibley's suicide have to do with any of this?"

"All we know for sure is that she had a bottle of those damned tranquilizers the doctor gave out. But don't go telling all this to Ellis. He's one of the few people in town who missed the bishop's court. That's when we all got together and decided he had enough on his mind without worrying about what was really happening on Doc's table."

"Did Doctor Joe leave a suicide note?"

"He had cancer."

"Sure," Traveler said. "A terminal case if I've ever heard of one."

The heat, a hundred and one degrees of it if the thermometer in front of Odell's Drug Store was to be believed, had turned the asphalt streets as sticky as old gum. By the time Traveler reached the motel, crossing its gravel parking area was like walking on hot coals. Each step brought fresh waves of mosquitoes up from Cowdery Creek to attack with kamikaze-like frenzy.

Slapping at his ears, he ran to the screen door. It was locked. Through it he could see Martin and Dora Neff staring at one another across the open space that separated the bungalow's twin beds. They looked as shy as lovers the morning after.

"I'm being eaten alive out here."

"Sorry," Martin said, coming to the rescue.

Once inside, Traveler ran cool water in the bathroom sink and bathed his face and hands. While he was drying himself, he explained the situation. "In case you haven't noticed, the wind has stopped. So as of now, the fire is static. Even so, the bishop has asked all the women to gather at the Co-op in case they have to be evacuated. I need to talk to one of them. Maybe more."

"The last time you were there they ran you out," Martin said.

"That's where Dora comes in."

"I don't like hiding behind a woman," Martin said.

"Don't be so old-fashioned," she told him. "That's why you brought me, isn't it?"

Ten minutes later Traveler and Martin were standing in front of the Co-op waiting for Dora to come out. They kept the Jeep's door open for a quick retreat. Underfoot, the street tar felt as if it were about to lose all surface tension.

Martin squatted and dug his fingers into the asphalt to collect a gummy ball. "I used to chew this stuff when I was a kid. Poor man's Wrigley's, we called it." He stood up, rolling the tar between his fingers.

"She's taking a long time," Traveler said.

Martin sniffed the tar ball. "Do you remember this one? 'My mamma gave me a penny to buy some candy. I didn't buy the candy, I bought some chewing gum. My mama gave me a nickel to buy a pickle. I didn't buy the pickle, I bought some chewing gum.'"

"You're not going to chew that, are you?"

"It's all right," Dora called from the Co-op's open door. "It's safe to come in."

A few feet inside the doorway, a quilting rack had been set up, blocking their way. A quilt, the same one Traveler had seen Mrs. Joe working on, effectively screened off the rest of the Co-op.

"This is the only way you're going to get your interview," Dora said. "Mrs. Colton's willing to speak with you, but not face to face. Not now that you know what happened to her."

"How can I be sure it's her I'm talking to?"

"I know her by sight," Dora said. "She's sitting on the other side right now. You have my word on it."

A metal folding chair stood at one end of the rack. Dora sat on it, taking hold of the quilt's edge like a net judge at a tennis match.

Joseph Smith had used a similar setup, hiding behind a blanket, when he translated *The Book of Mormon* from golden tablets using magic glasses supplied by the Angel Moroni.

"She says you may ask your questions," Dora said.

Traveler wondered how many women were listening on the other side. "Do you realize what happened to Claire Bennion?"

"She's nodding that she does," Dora said.

Martin rolled his eyes and leaned against the wall.

Traveler shook his head. He should have asked for two more chairs. "I need your help to find out who killed her. Before someone else gets hurt."

"She's nodding," Dora said. "She agrees."

Martin started chewing on something. Traveler hoped it wasn't road tar. A line went through his head. *My mother gave me a dime to buy a lime. I didn't buy the lime, I bought some chewing gum.*

"Let's start with Melba Nibley. Is there anything about her that you left out the first time we talked?"

Dora nodded.

"If I'd known who you were," Shirley Colton said, her voice calm, "I wouldn't have spoken to you at all."

"I apologize for misleading you."

"It doesn't matter anymore."

When she didn't continue, Dora smiled at one side of the quilt and then the other. Traveler concentrated on the pattern, tracing his past movements on the hand-sewn map of Wasatch. He'd reached the Uinta Hotel when the Colton woman continued.

"I don't know everything that went on, only what Melba told me. It's hard to remember it now, after so much has happened. She kept coming to see me every day. Each time she'd tell me something new and then get so embarrassed she'd have to leave. But the next day she'd be back, picking up the story and going forward with it until she couldn't face me anymore. Like me with you now, Mr. Traveler."

Traveler nodded. Dora picked up the movement and passed it on to the other side of the quilt.

"She never did come right out with it, what Doctor Joe had done to her. She kept beating around the bush. But I knew what she meant, all right, because I'd gone through it myself."

Traveler found the doctor's house on the map, remembered the rusting examination table, stirrups and all, that had been tossed out like junk.

"Melba felt she had betrayed her husband. 'I've committed adultery,' she said. I told her it was rape but she wouldn't believe me. She kept reading from our good book. 'If he murdered he was punished unto death; and if he committed adultery he was also punished.'"

The quilt bowed as if someone had touched it gently from the other side. "She got a rash and called it her punishment. She thought it was a venereal disease. I tried to tell her she was being foolish but she wouldn't listen. That it was nothing but hives. That if Doctor Joe had VD, half the women in town would be diseased. But nothing helped. She got hysterical and couldn't breathe. She got chest pains and I thought she was going to die. I wanted to call Ellis, but she didn't want me worrying her husband at work, so I took her to Doctor Joe's office. I figured even he was better than nothing in an emergency. Looking back on it, I thank God he wasn't there."

The quilt moved again, as if a finger were tracing a line across it.

"He was at a medical convention in Salt Lake, Mrs. Joe told us. So all she could do was lay hands upon Melba while we both prayed. When the pain kept up, Mrs. Joe went into her husband's office and found something for Melba to take. Whatever it was, it relaxed her right away. Probably the same tranquilizers he prescribed for all us women. Dear God, we made it easy for him. 'We don't want an attack of nerves,' he'd say. 'So take one capsule an hour before coming in to see me.' Like sheep, we'd do it."

She paused; her harsh breathing registered against the quilt. "Once I forgot to take mine, but even then I didn't realize what was happening, only that I was embarrassed because his examination seemed so much like sex with my husband. It took a stranger, another doctor in Salt Lake, to tell me what was actually going on."

The quilt trembled. "If it hadn't been for that," she said, "I'd still be going in there for my pelvics and letting him do it to me."

Without touching the quilt's surface, Traveler ran his finger parallel to Main Street, stopping at Odell's Drug Store. A hangman's noose had been stitched in black in the upper left-hand corner of the square representing the building. Doctor Joe's office, he remembered, was on the second floor.

"When Melba's chest pains stopped," Shirley Colton went on, her voice devoid of emotion, "Mrs. Joe said she should be anointed with oil for a true cure. 'Oil, the laying on of hands, and prayers. That's worth more than all the doctors in the world.' Mrs. Joe's own words. 'I'll do what's necessary to save her.' So I left Melba there, with Mrs. Joe. But the cure didn't take, because that night Melba killed herself. Ever since, Mrs. Joe has blamed herself."

Traveler waited a long time before breaking the silence. "Did Doctor Joe give you the tranquilizers personally?"

"At first he did. Free samples, he said, that he got from

the drug companies. But after a while he wrote prescriptions for us."

"For all his women patients here in town?"

Dora, blinded by tears, shook her head at Traveler.

"I can't vouch for that," Shirley Colton said.

"Can you vouch for the women who wrote to the State Medical Board?"

"Yes. They . . . we all took his tranquilizers. Like a bunch of foolish sheep to the slaughter."

"Are you certain that Ellis Nibley doesn't know any of this?"

"Of course."

For the first time, he didn't believe her.

He was about to pursue the matter when he heard footsteps on the other side of the quilt. The footsteps were followed by a whispered conversation. As soon as that ended, Shirley Colton spoke to him again. "The sheriff just called, checking to see if you were here, Mr. Traveler. He wants you to meet him at the Nibley place. He says it's an emergency."

Traveler parked across the street from the Nibley house. Except for the sheriff's car out front, the place looked as deserted as the first time he'd seen it. But then the entire town looked as if it had been abandoned to the fire.

He turned to Dora Neff, who was sitting in the back seat. Crying had left her eyes swollen, her nose red. Tears had uncovered deep wrinkles beneath her makeup.

"I hope you won't need me in there," she said. "A woman's presence would only embarrass the poor man."

"I agree," Martin said from the passenger's seat. "It's best that you talk to Nibley and the sheriff alone. But if you need us, you know where we'll be."

Humming his chewing gum song, Martin got out of the front seat and slid into the back beside Dora. "We'll be right here."

As Traveler walked up the overgrown path toward the house, he heard his father singing, "'My mother gave me a dollar to buy a collar. I didn't buy the collar, I bought some chewing gum.'"

The door jerked open before Traveler had time to use the heavy brass knocker. Ellis Nibley, wild-eyed and disheveled, stood there pointing a gun at Traveler's chest. Traveler risked a glance back toward the car, but his father was singing to Dora Neff and oblivious to the situation.

The revolver—a .357 by the looks of it, a twin of the one Sheriff Hickman wore—twitched, a movement meant to wave Traveler inside. He obeyed carefully. Nibley bolted the door behind them.

A narrow entrance hall, crammed with a turn-of-the-century hat rack and a massive marble-topped sideboard, opened into a parlor on one side, a dining room on the other. Sheriff Hickman was in the parlor, facedown on an oriental rug, blood oozing from a gash on the side of his bald head. He groaned when Traveler knelt beside him.

"Are you all right?"

"More or less."

"He may have a concussion," Traveler said for Nibley's benefit.

But the man, whose eyes were fixed and unblinking, didn't respond.

"What happened?" Traveler said.

Hickman rolled over and folded his hands on his chest as if preparing himself for burial. "Ask him. He called me. He told me to get you here and come myself. He said you were in danger."

Nibley backed against a Victorian armchair and sat down abruptly.

"Let me give you a hand," Traveler said to the sheriff.

Nibley shook his head sharply as if to clear his vision. "You'd better lay down there beside him, Mr. Traveler."

"You're not going to shoot anybody," Hickman said, pulling himself up to a sitting position with Traveler's help.

"Now put that gun down. I intend to sit on something more comfortable. Either that or I'm going to be sick."

He didn't wait for an answer, but slowly made his way across the room to a Victorian love seat upholstered in green velvet. Traveler settled onto a carpet-backed rocker.

Nibley laid the revolver in his lap but kept his hand wrapped around the grip, his forefinger curled inside the trigger guard. "I made a mistake hiring you, Mr. Traveler. I realize that now. That's why I asked you here. I want the sheriff to run you out of town."

"All you had to do was fire me. It would have been easier."

"You wouldn't have left, not after what happened to the Bennion woman."

"I told him that when I got here a few minutes ago," Hickman said. "That somebody was going to get hurt, probably me, if I tried running you out now."

"It's nice to know I have an ally," Traveler said.

"You don't." Hickman leaned back and closed his eyes. "I was about to tell Ellis I had a good reason for keeping you around, when he grabbed me." The sheriff cleared his throat. "I always prefer keeping an eye on the devil I know."

"Is that when he hit you?" Traveler asked.

"It was more of a scuffle. I lost my balance and fell and hit my head on the ottoman. That's when he took my gun." The sheriff touched a finger to his head wound, which was already clotting. His eyes opened to glare at Nibley. "I'm willing to forget all about this, Ellis, if you give me back my revolver, *now.*"

Nibley stared down at the weapon as if he'd never seen it before. When he looked up, his unblinking eyes fastened on Traveler's face. "I got a phone call. About what went on in Doctor Joe's office. I was never so embarrassed in my life, hearing things like that from women."

"Who called you?" Hickman said.

"I can't repeat such things." Nibley's trigger finger tightened.

Traveler rolled his eyes at the sheriff, trying to signal caution. But the man seemed oblivious.

"I don't know if it's true or not," the sheriff said. "Part of me wants to think it's mass hysteria or something like that. Whatever the case, it's over and done with. The man's dead."

Nibley twitched. "Dear God. Did everybody know about Doctor Joe but me?"

"I'm afraid so," Hickman said.

Nibley jerked up his arm, extending it until the .357 was pointing at the sheriff's chest. The weight of the weapon made his arm tremble. At a range of ten feet the shakes wouldn't matter.

Nibley said, "Why wasn't I told what he did to my Melba? I could have saved her."

"I didn't know then," the sheriff responded. "Like I said, I still don't know for sure. But we agreed at the Bishop's Court not to cause you any more suffering."

"If you'd told me, I'd never have called in an outsider, a Gentile. You, Mr. Traveler."

The .357 swung in Traveler's direction. "The longer you stay here, the more stories will spread about my wife. All my customers at the store will know. I won't be able to face them. I—"

"Dammit, man," the sheriff interrupted, "you can't undo what's already done."

Jesus, Traveler thought. That was no way to talk to a man holding a gun.

Hickman stood up, patting his gun belt and winking at Traveler. "It's time to stop playing games, Ellis."

The knocker banged against the front door. Nibley twitched so badly Traveler expected the gun to go off.

"Who's that?" Nibley said, swinging the .357 around to aim at the sound.

My father, Traveler answered to himself, and launched himself at Nibley. The Victorian chair shattered under the impact of his two hundred and twenty pounds. Nibley screamed. His eyes rolled up into his head.

"Goddammit," Hickman muttered. "I was trying to tell you it wasn't loaded. I never load my gun around town."

"Why the hell didn't you say so?"

"Couldn't you see there were no bullets in the chambers?"

Traveler didn't answer, didn't have to. They both knew the rule. Approach all guns as if they're loaded.

"All I wanted to do was keep him talking," the sheriff said. "To hear what he had to say for himself."

As gently as possible, Traveler removed the broken chair from beneath the unconscious man. The movement, though slight, pushed a piece of bloody collarbone through Nibley's shirt.

"Keep him quiet, Traveler. I'm going to call Mrs. Joe. She's the closest we've got to a nurse here in town."

"Send my father for her. It will be faster."

Ten minutes later, Mrs. Joe walked in, took one look at Nibley groaning on the floor where he'd fallen, and went to her knees. She bowed her head momentarily before laying hands upon him and anointing him with oil from the small flask around her neck. She began at his forehead and worked her way down to his wound. The application quieted him almost immediately.

"What's happening to our town?" she murmured as her hands caressed the area where the bone had broken. Her starched nurse's uniform made crinkling noises. "We were like a single family once, before evil came among us."

She raised her head to stare Traveler in the eye. He had the feeling that she was looking right through him, at a vision discernible only to herself.

"I blame myself," she said.

"Why?" Traveler asked softly.

"I could have come to Ellis sooner, taken him by the hand, and healed his soul."

"Let's worry about him here and now," the sheriff said.

"The break isn't a clean one," she said. "The pain will return if you don't get him to the hospital in Ephraim immediately. You can take me home on the way."

Traveler and Hickman carried Nibley to the sheriff's cruiser, while Mrs. Joe walked alongside, her trembling hands on the stricken man. Once they'd laid him on the back seat, she climbed in the front.

Before closing the door, Mrs. Joe looked at Traveler and said, "I have seen the devil in the flesh."

As soon as the sheriff drove away, Traveler went over to the Jeep where his father and a frightened Dora Neff were waiting. He wanted them both out of Wasatch.

"For once don't argue," he said. "Just go."

Traveler felt shaken by the knowledge that he'd come close to killing Ellis Nibley, that he'd wanted to kill him for aiming the gun in Martin's direction.

"I'm supposed to be covering your back, remember?" Martin said.

Traveler shook his head.

"Okay. I know that look. At least let me stay with you until the sheriff gets back."

"I'll be fine. Once you're gone, I'll be the only man left in town."

"A woman could have killed Claire."

"Not by herself."

"You're on foot," Martin said.

"I don't have far to walk."

"Where are you going?"

"To see a woman about the devil."

Martin sighed and started the engine. Once the car was out of sight, Traveler walked to the corner and turned west on Heber Avenue. A block later he was standing in front of Doctor Joe's house. Despite the hundred-degree temperature, heavy smoke was pouring from the chimney, adding to the haze from the forest fire.

On the way up the front walk, Traveler detoured around the side of the house to where the abandoned examination table stood. The metal fittings, especially around the stirrups, were beginning to rust. He ran his hand over the table's padded leather top. It had been recently scrubbed, with a cleanser rough enough to discolor the surface.

He touched the stirrups, thought of the women who'd lain there, vulnerable women like Claire.

He pounded his fist into the leather. Questions filled his mind. Questions he should have asked Claire when she was alive. Things about her that were now gone forever.

He backed away from the examination table, from the images it cast, and returned to the front of the house. The door stood wide open. He stepped inside, felt the sucking draft of hot air rush past him, and followed the breeze into the living room, where it was fanning a fierce blaze in the fireplace.

In the center of the stifling room, Mrs. Joe was kneeling on an oval hearth rug, surrounded by stacks of manila folders. She must have felt a change in the air current, because she swung around, a startled look on her face. Her surprise gave way to a smile when she saw who it was.

After a moment, she turned her back on him and continued to feed folders into the fire.

"You told me you had your husband's records cremated along with the body," Traveler said.

"I lied."

He stepped forward to save what he could.

"It doesn't matter," she said when he pulled her to her feet. "Only the men are left. I burned the women this morning."

She twisted out of his grasp and reached into the front of her sooty uniform. When her hand reappeared, it held her phial of anointing oil.

With a sharp jerk, she snapped the chain and held the half-empty phial up before her eyes. Smiling, she unscrewed its golden cap. When the vessel was open, she refocused on Traveler. Her smile widened. She doused him with the clear liquid, then backed toward the fireplace, her eyes staring as if she expected him to disintegrate. When he didn't, her smile faded.

"Did you think I was the devil?" he said.

"I had to be sure." She sagged. The breath went out of her. "I've already met him once and cast him out."

Stepping to her side, he grabbed hold of her bare arms, lifted her away from the flames, and carried her to one of the pewlike benches that had once held Doctor Joe's waiting patients. When he put her down, she rubbed her arms where his fingers had been. Out of the corner of his eye he noticed an empty quilt rack standing in one corner of the room. It hadn't been there on his previous visit.

"Tell me about the devil," he said, standing over her, intimidating her with his size, implying a threat of violence.

Without looking at him, Mrs. Joe stopped rubbing her arms and began hugging herself.

"Answer me."

Her head came up. Her eyes widened, staring beyond him with such intensity that he glanced over his shoulder to make certain they were still alone.

She said, "*The Book of Mormon* tells us everything we

need to know. 'They who are filthy are the devil and his angels; and they shall go away into everlasting fire.'"

She twisted sideways to peer around him at the fireplace. He moved so she had nothing to look up at but him.

"He's there," she said, nodding as if she could see right through Traveler. "In the flames, burning. I can smell him. I can . . ."

Her chin sank onto her breast. "God forgive me. Part of me loves him still."

"I know all about your husband," he said.

"Are they telling everyone now, even Gentiles?"

"Claire Bennion gives me the right to know."

Her head tilted back, stretching her neck almost to the breaking point so she could look him in the eye. What she saw made her squirm.

"Tell me about Claire," he said.

Her eyelids fluttered before closing down completely. "All those years I knew something was wrong. I sensed it. But I made excuses to myself each time we'd lose a female patient to the doctor over in Ephraim. I'd think, 'It's a personality conflict, that's all. Nothing more. Nothing to do with Doctor Joe.'"

Her breath caught so suddenly she gasped. "I tried to be professional. I told myself that I was a nurse first, not a wife. That it was wrong for me to listen to any of the rumors, or feel any kind of jealousy toward my husband's patients. But I should have listened to my heart. I should never have left him alone to examine those women."

"Why did you?"

"He said they'd be embarrassed being examined in front of someone they grew up with. Pelvics were private, he kept telling me, something between doctor and patient. I wanted to believe him. I tried to believe him."

Her eyes opened; her head snapped sideways hard enough to send tears flying.

"Claire," he prompted, settling onto the other end of the bench, keeping his distance.

Mrs. Joe sneaked a look at him before ducking her head. "She was only a child when she came to us the first time. Thirteen or fourteen. Even then she was on the verge of womanhood. Men were already looking at her the way they do. Thinking back on it, I must have seen that. I must have known there was no need to give a girl of virgin age a pelvic. Certainly not a dilation. But when she left in tears, in pain, I knew that had been the case. She was just starting high school, here to take a physical exam for gym class. You know the kind, to make sure she didn't have a heart problem, or anything that might make strenuous exercise dangerous."

"Claire had a child when she was in high school," he said.

Her hands pressed against her ears.

"I'm told that Doctor Joe arranged for the adoption."

She shook her head.

"The baby died," he said.

Her hands fell away. "You should have seen my husband's baby pictures. They'd been hand colored to show his fine soft red hair." She pointed to the empty frames on the mantel. "I burned them, all of his pictures."

"The Beasleys' son has red hair," Traveler said.

"Do you think I'm blind?" Defiance flared in her voice, abetted by a thin joyless smile. "I'm stepmother to God knows how many children."

"You could have saved them," he said, "the ones like Claire. You could have been there when she tried to tell her father what happened. You could have stopped him from throwing her out."

"I did my best. I kept track of her child until he died."

"Tell me about him."

"The records are burned."

Traveler grabbed her wrist, squeezing too hard, not being able to help himself, stopping only when she whimpered.

Ashamed, he said, "I'm sorry."

She began rocking back and forth. Her eyes were unblinking, fearful, staring at the fireplace as if hell were opening up for her.

"Do you think children pay for the sins of their mothers?" she asked.

"I hope not."

"What about a wife like me?"

Traveler said nothing.

"A wife who denied Melba Nibley when she came to me for help. 'You're being hysterical,' I told her, denying what I'd secretly known to be true for years. 'Forgive me,' she said, 'I have sinned with your husband.' The poor, shamed woman. She thought she was alone, the only sinner among his patients."

"Rape is not a victim's sin," he said.

"I dreamed about Melba that night," Mrs. Joe went on. "I saw her up in the stirrups. I saw . . . You can imagine what I saw. The next day, I checked my husband's records while he was busy with other patients. I counted pelvics against the reason for the office visits. They didn't match the patients' symptoms."

She looked beyond him, her unblinking eyes dripping tears. "Still, I had to be certain, didn't I? I had to see for myself. My chance came with a young girl, seventeen and naive, new in town, who was about to be married in the Manti temple. She was a lunch hour patient, working summers to save honeymoon money and unable to see Doctor during regular office hours. I prepared the examination room as always, the sanitary paper cover on the table, the modesty drape, the dilators. I saw her in, waited for her to disrobe, helped her up onto the table, into the stirrups, arranged the drape, and then left the room when Doctor entered, like always. Only I didn't close the door all the way. I left it ajar so I could listen. 'And when is the wedding to be, my dear?' 'Two weeks, Doctor Joe.' Her voice was slow and slurred by the tranquilizer. 'We'll have to see if we can help you then, won't we?' 'This is my first pelvic, doctor. I—' 'Yes, I know. I've studied your records, but there are more questions I have to ask. Try not to be embarrassed.' 'Yes, Doctor.' 'Have you had relations before, with a man?'"

Mrs. Joe's face shone with sweat. Her bulging eyes reminded Traveler of a deep-sea fish brought to the surface too quickly. "'No, Doctor,' she told my husband. 'I've saved myself for marriage.' 'Well then, it's my job to help you along, isn't it? To get you ready for your husband by taking away the pain and turning it into a purrrrr.'"

Mrs. Joe stretched out the last word until breath failed her. She had to pant before continuing. "'Now relax, dear,' he said. The bastard. 'I'll try not to be too rough.' 'What are you doing, Doctor? It hurts.' 'That's a special instrument you're feeling. We call it a dilator. It's designed to stretch you a little at a time. We begin with a small dilator and increase the size until we approximate your husband. I do this for all the young women who come to see me. It helps them on their wedding night.' 'It hurts, Doctor.' 'Just a little more, then I'll switch dilators. Each one should be a little easier.'"

Mrs. Joe groaned. But her eyes, her facial expression didn't change. "That's when I opened the door. It squeaked, but Doctor didn't notice. He was extracting the dilator with one hand, unzipping with the other. I wanted to scream, to stop him then and there before anything happened. But I couldn't. I knew it would be the end of us if I did. The end of our marriage. Though it already was. I just wasn't thinking it through. All I did was stand there and watch. He's a big man, you know. Triple the dilator. Quadruple. Even the tip, the glans, made her cry. He stopped immediately, holding himself there at the ready, wheedling her. 'We can't stop now, dear. Think of your wedding night.' The girl was clutching at the table, trying to back away, but the stirrups held her, kept her fully exposed the way they're designed to. 'All right?' 'I'll try, Doctor.' 'Good, dear. Take a deep breath. It won't hurt for long.' 'Oh. Oh, please, stop. I beg you.'"

Mrs. Joe wrapped her arms around her thighs, hugging them together so tightly she trembled. "He couldn't stop, of course. He was too far gone. When it was over, I closed the door. Not hard, you understand. Just enough to let Doctor know I'd been there, watching him."

She glanced toward the open door as if expecting to see the doctor again. When she didn't, she slipped off the bench to kneel in front of the dying fire, feeding it more files to bring it back to life.

"When I confronted him later," she said, looking into the flames, "he told me I was to blame because I couldn't have children. He said I was inadequate as a woman." She shook her head from side to side as if denying the words. "All those nights I'd waited for him. But he never came. He never touched me. Not in years."

She hurled folders into the fire, keeping it up until the flames leapt into the chimney, until she'd exhausted her supply of fuel. The heat finally drove her back to the bench, bringing with her a smell of singed hair.

"It's all over now," she said quietly.

"Not yet," he said.

"There's nothing left but ashes."

Traveler closed his eyes; his mind went back to Sunday school in the basement of the ward house. He saw the chairs in a semicircle around the teacher, heard her read from *The Book of Mormon*. He followed along with her, out loud for Mrs. Joe's benefit. "'And those who would not confess their sins and repent of their iniquity, the same were not numbered among the people of the church, and their names were blotted out.'"

"I know what you want from me, but nothing—not even confession—will bring Claire back to you."

She peered into his eyes.

"I spoke with her kidnapper on the phone," he said. "It was a woman's voice. You."

"I testified before the Bishop's Court. I damned my own husband to hell. The day before he died they excommunicated him."

"Are you telling me that's why he killed himself?"

"Looking at you, Mr. Traveler, I don't think you're a Gentile at all. Your eyes have a burning in them, like the faithful, like I used to see in myself in the morning mirror." She sighed. "Have you been sent here to forgive me?"

Not trusting his voice, he nodded once, stiffly.

"To help me atone for my sins?"

Another nod, so rigid his neck muscles creaked.

"You know the answers already, Mr. Traveler. That's what I think."

He bowed his head to keep his doubting eyes away from her.

"Doctor Joe drank coffee, you know. He said he needed the boost it gave him to start the day. 'The devil's boost,' I used to say to him. I said it again when he drank his last cup, the one I put the tranquilizers in. Enough capsules to be sure he wouldn't have the strength to fight back. But not so many that he'd lose consciousness."

She paused, craning her neck to stare at the ceiling. He followed her gaze to the heavy wooden cross-beams that supported the steeply pitched roof. Scrape marks showed where something, possibly a rope, had scoured away the paint.

"I fetched a ladder from the garage and rigged a block and tackle up there. Doctor was lying right here on the hearth rug. I raised his head and wrapped a towel around his neck so the rope wouldn't cut into him, so no blood would spill. So there'd be no atonement for his sins. So that he could never be raised from the dead."

Traveler swallowed sharply. His imagination felt the rope drag him off his feet, haul him up slowly, cut off his air for a long time dying. "Claire," he said. "I want to know about her."

"Her blood was spilled. Her sins are washed away."

She glanced at the door, but he wouldn't be distracted.

"You could never have handled a woman like Claire on your own," he said. "Not unless you drugged her too."

"We . . . I didn't want to hurt her."

Traveler stood up, casting his shadow on her instead of striking out as he longed to do. "Who?" he repeated, clenching his fists in her face.

"Go ahead and kill me," she said. "It would be a blessing. Send me to hell with Doctor Joe."

Looking at the woman, Traveler knew there was nothing he could do to her. Nothing worse than what she was doing to herself. His hands dropped to his sides. He turned his back on her to seek the open door. That's when he saw Shirley Colton standing there on the threshold, a folded quilt in her arms. She looked frightened.

"I . . . I brought the quilt for Mrs. Joe. She said she wanted to work on it."

She hurried past him and began spreading the quilt over the rack in the corner of the living room. It was the same quilt he'd seen at the Co-op, with its hand-stitched map of Wasatch, street by street and building by building.

Mrs. Joe brushed Traveler aside to get her sewing box from the mantel. She rummaged inside it for a moment before handing a needle and spool to Shirley Colton.

"Will you thread it for me, dear? I can't seem to focus my eyes for close-up work just now."

Mrs. Colton wet the end of the thread several times be-

fore succeeding. When she handed over the needle and
thread, Mrs. Joe began sewing on the quilt immediately.

Traveler moved close enough to see the subject of her
needlework. It was Odell's Drug Store.

"Just about every woman in town has worked on this
quilt at one time or another," Mrs. Colton said. "Everything
is there to see if you know what to look for."

Mrs. Joe's needle moved in and out of the material
rapidly, outlining what looked like a half-circle.

"What else has to be done?" Traveler asked.

"This is the finishing touch," she said. "As far as the
quilt is concerned."

Traveler watched silently as the half-circle evolved into a
skull. Finally, Mrs. Joe sighed and stepped back to admire
her work.

"Do you think it should be a plain skull, Shirley, or a
skull and crossbones?"

"Whatever you want, dear."

Mrs. Joe went back to work, adding bones. "Enos Odell
came to me," she said, her head inches from the quilt.
"Everybody in town was blaming him, he said, because he'd
filled Doctor Joe's tranquilizer prescriptions. I felt sorry for
Enos. I was a fool."

Traveler studied the quilt. A great many details had been
added since he'd first seen Norma Beasley working on it at
the motel. He wondered how complete a history it was, if it
might even contain an image of himself. The angel he'd seen
at the Co-op, the one of his namesake, Moroni, now looked
like the Angel of Death.

"Enos said we had to run you out of town," Mrs. Joe said.
"Otherwise things would never be right again. He showed
me a newspaper clipping from a Salt Lake paper. It was about
you and your girlfriend, Claire Bennion. It said you did crazy
things to protect her. So all we had to do, Enos figured, was
pretend to kidnap her and you'd do whatever we wanted.

Even then I told him no. But he said if I didn't help him, he'd make sure Doctor Joe's story got in the newspapers too."

"You killed her," he said.

Mrs. Joe reached out to Shirley Colton for support, but the woman sidestepped out of the way.

Mrs. Joe held on to the quilt rack. "I should have remembered about Enos. But I didn't. I followed his instructions and drove over to Moroni to see Claire. She didn't remember me at first. Of course a lot of years had passed since she was a patient, and I wasn't wearing my uniform either that night. People see the uniform, you know, not the person. Anyway, when she heard what we had planned for you—threatening you on the phone and telling you we'd kidnapped her—she came along with me just like Enos said she would. It was a big joke to her. She was laughing and telling stories about you on the ride back here."

She looked at Mrs. Colton, who'd begun to cry.

"But when I turned into my driveway, Claire saw the old examination table in the headlights. She saw the stirrups. That's when she remembered me and started shouting at me. I tried to calm her down. All she had to do, I said, was call you like she'd done so many times before. That we'd let her go then. God knows, I thought it was the truth."

Feeling weak in the knees, Traveler sat on the nearest bench.

"That's when everything went wrong. Enos came out of the house and grabbed her. She smelled him, his druggist's smell, and went crazy. He hit her to shut her up. When I tried to stop him, he hit me too."

Mrs. Joe touched her breast to show where Odell's blows had fallen. "There's a back door to my husband's office, with an outside stairway leading up to it. That door opened during her first pelvic all those years ago, Claire told me while we were tying her up. She'd felt the draft and smelled Enos. 'You're nothing but a pervert,' she screamed at him. 'A peeper who's good for nothing except watching other people do it.'"

Traveler swallowed, remembering the man's smell, how unforgettable it was.

"The moment I heard her, I knew it was true. I knew he'd been watching with every woman in town." Mrs. Joe sighed. "You see, he'd been caught playing Peeping Tom before. Not in Doctor Joe's office, but in his own neighborhood. He came to the church then and asked for forgiveness. We prayed with him, and took him at his word when he said he was saved."

She looked at Shirley Colton, who nodded confirmation.

"When Sheriff Mahonri caught him at it a second time," Mrs. Joe went on, "we shunned him. He and Cynthia both, since it's a wife's duty to stay with her husband for better or worse."

She shuddered. Mrs. Colton went to her then, hugging her, trying to comfort her.

"Anyway, when your Claire called Enos a Peeping Tom," Mrs. Joe continued, "I saw the devil come into his eyes. He hit her again, so hard I panicked and ran out of the house. I haven't seen him since, except to talk to on the phone. He called the next day to gloat about killing her. To tell me how he'd done it in the old Mormon way. People would blame the Nibley brothers, he said, because they'd had trouble with you already. Because everybody knew the Nibleys were hunters who liked to kill. Who tied their trophies to the fenders of their trucks and paraded through town."

"The Nibleys have an alibi," Traveler said.

"'They're bullies,' Enos kept saying. 'Nobody likes them.'"

She nodded at the memory. "'Bullies are cowards at heart,' I told him. 'The sheriff knows that. Your plan won't work.' But he wouldn't listen. He was crazy. He laughed and said I had to keep quiet because I was his accomplice. He said he'd kill me too if need be. 'Go ahead,' I told him. 'I'm in hell already.'"

"There, there," Mrs. Colton crooned. "We'll go to the Co-op and alert the others. They'll know what has to be done."

Mrs. Joe shook her head. "First we've got to bring Cynthia Odell back into the fold."

"Of course we do. A wife's loyalty goes only so far. If she joins us, her shunning's over."

The door to Odell's Drug Store stood open. Traveler
pressed his face against the front window. Enos Odell was
behind the soda fountain setting out bandages and medicine
on the marble countertop. He didn't look up, didn't see
Traveler staring at him.

Traveler stepped back onto the curb to study the Wasatch
Mountains. The fire line looked smaller to him. The smoke
was definitely thinning.

He drew a deep breath of relatively fresh air and went
inside, closing the door behind him and throwing the dead
bolt.

Odell jumped at the sound. "I'm sorry," he said as soon
as he saw who it was. "We're not open for anything but
emergencies."

Traveler walked slowly along the counter, spinning the
stools as he went, and examining the array of medical supplies. In addition to sterile pads, bandages, and tape, there

were jars of salve and bottles of painkillers. Even a brand-name tranquilizer.

Traveler swung onto a stool and stared the druggist in the eye.

After a few seconds of silence, Odell began rearranging the clutter on the countertop, lining up bottles and bandages, busywork to escape Traveler's scowl.

"The bishop sent me here," Odell said in a rush, as if compelled to fill the silence. "Off the fire line to get things ready in case someone's hurt and needs first aid."

Traveler didn't answer, didn't blink.

"I've just about got everything ready, so if there's something you need, tell me. Maybe something cold to drink, a phosphate? Better yet, a malt?"

He didn't wait for a response, but began scooping ice cream into a metal container. "Vanilla? Chocolate? Let's make it chocolate. That's my favorite."

He added syrup, a teaspoon of malt, and milk to the ice cream. "Maybe a little more malt. What do you think?" He nodded at his own suggestion, added another spoonful, and attached the metal container to the mixer.

While it whirred, he cleared counter space in front of Traveler, removing the tranquilizers along with several other tablet-filled jars. All went out of sight beneath the counter.

When the malt was ready, he poured it into a tall glass and placed it in front of Traveler. "You won't get anything like this in Salt Lake."

"Those tranquilizers," Traveler said. "Were those the ones Doctor Joe prescribed?"

"I don't know what you mean."

"The bishop didn't send you here to get ready for emergencies. He sent you away."

"What do you mean?"

Traveler looked at his watch. "The word has spread by now. They know about you. What you did to Claire."

Odell shuddered.

"I know the feeling," Traveler said. "Like somebody stepped on your grave."

"I never touched any of them."

"You touched Claire."

Odell tried to back up, but the ice cream freezer stopped him.

"How many tranquilizers would it take to kill a man?" Traveler asked.

The druggist shook his head. "You can't make me do it."

"Do you think I'm just going to walk away?"

"She . . . she laughed at me."

"You butchered her like an animal."

"I'm a Temple Mormon. I know my scripture. I follow it to the letter. I killed her in the Mormon way. It's my only hope of salvation."

Traveler caught movement out of the corner of his eye. He sought its source in the mirror behind the counter. Shirley Colton was at the door, her face distorted against the glass. One hand held an axe, new by the look of it, the same kind he'd seen at her hardware store. She rattled the door handle. The lock held.

Odell glanced toward the back door.

"Mrs. Joe called the Relief Society," Traveler said. "She told them everything."

Another woman arrived out front. She, too, carried an axe.

Odell began edging toward the rear of the store. Traveler was about to cut him off, when someone began pounding on the back door. The druggist stopped, swung around, and went wide-eyed.

Traveler followed his terrified gaze. Women's faces filled the front window. Louise Dority. The five Mrs. McConkies. Norma Beasley. Even Hope Doyle, the town Catholic. Plus at least a dozen he didn't recognize. All carried tools, apparently from Colton's Hardware. Axes, hoes, rakes, weeders. They began tapping on the glass in a persistent cadence, not hard enough to break it, but getting louder and louder just the same.

"Please," Odell said.

Traveler nodded at the front door, where the druggist's wife now stood. She was fitting a key into the lock with one hand and holding a baseball bat in the other.

Traveler slid off the stool and started toward the back door. "I think you're about to be called home."

Traveler stood at his office window looking out at the temple. The weather had changed. The Angel Moroni was hidden in a low rain cloud, part of a storm front that had come boiling across the Great Salt Lake the day after Traveler returned from Wasatch. An inch of rain had fallen so far, unusual so early in the fall. God's intervention, some called it, because the downpour had extinguished the forest fires burning in the mountains above Salt Lake.

The phone rang. He sat down before answering it.

"This is Stacie Breen," a woman said. She sounded young, Claire's age. "My boyfriend said you called while I was at work."

He'd gotten the name from Dora Neff, who'd found it in one of Claire's letters. *She's a good friend,* Claire had written, her only mention of another woman. *You can trust her.*

"I was calling about Claire Bennion," he said.

"I know. She told me about you. She said you'd come for her one day." Her voice caught. "It's too late now, isn't it?"

"I'm looking for her little boy."

"You know what she called you, don't you? Her Angel Moroni."

"She did have a child, didn't she?"

"I could deny it," the woman said.

"Are you?"

"With Claire gone, there's no reason to. She can't get into any more trouble."

"Where is he?" Traveler asked.

"She named him after you, you know."

"She told me."

"It's not my fault what happened."

Traveler swung around to face the window, looking for the real Angel Moroni, but the statue was still hidden in cloud.

"I couldn't help the boy myself. I have my own life to worry about."

"Are you trying to tell me he's dead?"

"Nothing like that. She gave him away."

"Adoption?"

"No papers were signed, if that's what you mean."

"What then?"

"She got money, though she wouldn't tell me how much."

"Tell me where he is. Please."

"I don't know. That's the truth. All she'd say was that she gave him away so that you'd be sure to come looking for her."

He closed his eyes.

"For her and your son," the woman added.

"Is there anything else you can tell me?"

"He's in southern Utah somewhere, I think. At least that's the impression she gave me. Are you going to look for him?"

Traveler thanked her and hung up, wondering if Stacie

Breen wasn't part of one last game Claire was playing on him. One last fruitless search.

He was still mulling that over when his father came through the door, carrying a soggy brown paper bag under one arm and an equally soggy newspaper under the other. Once both were deposited on Traveler's desk, Martin shrugged out of his raincoat and dropped it on the client's chair.

"I mailed back Ellis Nibley's fee," Traveler said.

"That means I'll be paying the rent again this month." Martin shook his head and began rummaging in a filing cabinet. "Got ya," he said after a moment. He held up a stack of paper cups, separated out two, and filled them from the whiskey bottle inside the decomposing paper bag.

"What are we celebrating?" Traveler asked.

Martin raised his cup. "I read it in the newspaper. This storm front goes all the way to Sanpete County. The fires are out in Wasatch too."

Traveler drank until his eyes watered.

"One casualty was reported," Martin added. "A man named Enos Odell. They said he was killed while fighting the fire."